I0822785

Crests of Magic

Jordan Kapp

eBook ISBN: 979-8-90254-996-3
Paperback ISBN: 979-8-90254-995-6
Hardcover ISBN: 979-8-90254-994-9

Contents

Chapter 1

Walkways stretched across the skyline like silver threads, connecting the floating districts to the streets of Salt Lake City below. Emric Vale adjusted the strap of his backpack as he and his younger sister stepped onto one of the low-altitude lifts carrying students toward their skybound school. His ash-brown hair was tousled by the breeze, and his pale blue eyes scanned the horizon with quiet uncertainty. Above them, the morning sun glinted off the suspended districts, clusters of homes, shops, and gardens that hovered lazily in the air like anchored clouds.

"You're quiet," Nia said, looking up from the glowing pamphlet in her hand. Her straight light-brown hair caught the morning sun, and her green eyes flicked toward him with curiosity.

"More than usual, even."

Emric didn't answer right away. The lift jerked slightly as it rose, giving them a sweeping view of the Great Salt Lake. Magic shimmered on its surface like steam rising from a frying pan. He would have to get used to that in this city. It wasn't like New York, where magic pulsed through the buildings and roared in every alley. This place breathed magic slowly, like it was still adjusting to the weight of it.

"New school. New people," Emric muttered. "And I haven't picked my domain yet. I'm sixteen, Nia. What are they going to think when they find out the new kid still hasn't picked a domain?"

She folded the pamphlet with a snap and stuffed it into her bag. "They'll think you're interesting. Maybe even mysterious."

Emric let out a hollow laugh. "You've always been a terrible liar."

Nia grinned. "Only when I want to be."

The lift reached the top, depositing them at a landing dock suspended just above the city's historical district. From here, narrow skybridges wove through the air, linking floating gardens, winding courtyards, and the ever-present spires of their new school in the sky: Cloudrest Academy, a sleek silver-and-bronze structure held aloft by a ring of glowing pylons. It was a sharp contrast to his old school in New York, which sat firmly on the ground and looked like it belonged in a museum. This one seemed pulled straight out of a Protoss base from StarCraft.

Below, Salt Lake City buzzed with life. Enchanted trams zipped along mana rails.

Commuters tapped their Fluxbags on payment plates. In the far distance, the jagged edge of the Wasatch Mountains cut the horizon like the crest of a sleeping giant.

Somewhere among the bustle, Kael, Emric and Nia's older brother, was already at work. Far behind them, their father still hadn't gotten out of bed. The apartment was still stacked with unopened moving boxes.

"Just be yourself," Nia said with a laugh. "Stop worrying about what other people will think. She gave him a playful nudge. "That's what Mom would've told you, right?"

That put a slight smile on Emric's face as they crossed the final skybridge toward the soaring gates of Highveil Hall.

The glass doors hissed open with a soft magical hum. There was great power in these halls; Emric couldn't see it, but he could feel it pressing on his chest like a weight. The air inside was cool and faintly floral, touched with the steady thrum of enchantments.

Magic glowed subtly in the walls, guiding lights, floating directories, even self-sorting filing cabinets that shuffled papers in midair.

"Hey, Emric," Nia said, tugging him toward the receptionist's desk. The aged woman behind it looked up politely.

"Names?"

"Nia and Emric Vale," Nia said brightly, stepping forward.

A feathered quill scribbled their names across a glowing sheet of parchment. A moment later, the names vanished, replaced by lines of shifting magical text that the receptionist scanned quickly. A small smile touched her lips.

"Ah, transfer students."

Emric stiffened like a board. His face turned the color of boiled beetroot, and he blurted, “YES, MA’AM!” far louder than he intended.

The receptionist grinned and shook her head with faint amusement. With a flick of her wrist, two envelopes wrapped in shimmering glyphs floated toward them.

“These contain your class schedules, mana-alignment tags, and a map of the school.

Don’t lose your tags; your instructors will need to verify them before every session.”

Nia snatched hers effortlessly. “Thank you!”

Emric fumbled his and nearly dropped it. As he steadied the envelope, he noticed the nameplate on the desk: Haylee Atkinson.

The receptionist adjusted her glasses. “Miss Vale, you’ll be in Foundational Year III. Oh, it looks like you’re in the advanced track,” she added, impressed. “Your first class is with Professor Grenlyn in Skyroom 32.”

She turned to Emric next, still smiling, but her smile faltered slightly as she read his file, just enough for him to notice. After a quiet pause, she resumed professionally:

“Mister Vale, you’ll report to Room 41.”

Emric bowed awkwardly. “YES, MA’AM!” Again, the words came out far too loud.

Nia laughed softly. "You'll do fine." She gave him a wink, then darted up the stairs toward the advanced track.

Emric stood there for a moment, unsure whether to follow her or just dissolve into vapor on the spot.

Mrs. Atkinson tilted her head. "Was there something else I could help you with?"

"N-no, ma'am." Emric turned on his heel and stepped into the main hall of Cloudrest Academy.

Around him, students buzzed in every direction, some alone, some in pairs, many trailed by glowing familiars or floating notebooks that hovered like loyal pets.

Emric glanced at his schedule and took a slow, deep breath.

Okay. You've got this.

It's just a new school… with floating buildings.

He turned toward his homeroom and started walking.

Three Years Ago

The schoolyard in New York buzzed with magical energy as young mages flipped through new spellbooks, botched their first elemental drills, and struggled to read from freshly inscribed scrolls. Most fumbled through their exercises like kids trying to play the piano with mittens, technically managing it but barely.

One of the older students, a local blowhard with a mean streak, decided to have a little fun. With a smirk, he raised his hand and fired off an arcane bolt, crackling and fast.

He didn't aim at anyone, only an open patch of training ground. He wanted chaos—noise, dust, flying debris. Something to make the younger kids jump.

But before the bolt could land, before the instructors even turned, it stopped. Dead in the air. Frozen mid-flight.

Gasps rippled across the field.

The bolt hadn't dissipated or exploded. It hung suspended, humming, as stable as if it had been locked in place by invisible hands.

And at the center of the silence stood a boy.

Emric Vale

One hand raised, eyes wide with quiet focus, as if he didn't fully understand what he had just done.

He hadn't cast the spell. But somehow, he'd stopped it.

He didn't think. Didn't plan. He just reacted.

Back in the Present

Emric hovered just outside the classroom door, his fingers tightening around the strap of his bag. Voices echoed inside: laughing, teasing, someone dramatically recounting what sounded like a magical mishap involving a scroll, a goose, and a small explosion.

Emric took a deep breath.

You've done harder things than this, he told himself.

He opened the door and crossed the threshold.

The room carried that unmistakable magical-school scent: old scrolls, faint mana residue, and whatever potion the janitors used to clean. It was shaped like an amphitheater, with tiered seating wrapping around a raised demonstration platform.

Glowing blue and green runes floated above the podium where the professor would stand. A skeletal owl perched in the corner, hooting and ruffling its bony wings despite not having feathers.

Emric caught the attention of a few students near the entrance.

One of them made a beeline for him and offered a hand. "Hello! Welcome to Cloudrest

Academy. I'm Tamlin, the peer leader for the class, and it is my solemn duty to welcome you on your first day."

Tamlin was a bit taller than Emric, with a sturdy build that suggested he played mageball or something equally competitive. He had neatly combed brown hair, square glasses perched on his nose, and warm brown eyes that sparkled with an almost exhausting level of enthusiasm.

Emric was taken aback by the enthusiasm, but also appreciative. "Thank you," he said, placing his hand on the back of his head, unsure of exactly how to respond.

"Of course," Tamlin replied cheerfully. "Come along, Emric. Let me take you to your seat!" He said, immediately turning on his heel and marching off at a brisk pace.

Caught off guard by the speed of Tamlin's march, Emric jogged to catch up.

Tamlin stopped beside an empty spot in the amphitheater seating and motioned for Emric to sit. Tamlin took the seat next to him. "Even though we don't have desks, we still have assigned seating," he said, as if the idea still amused him after weeks. "We have a few minutes before the professor comes in—tell me, have you picked your domain yet?"

A bit embarrassed, Emric replied, "Not yet. I'm not sure what direction I want to go."

"Wonderful!" Tamlin said with genuine sincerity. "You're not the only one. A couple of students in the class haven't picked theirs either."

Emric stared in surprise. "Really?" Relief washed over him.

"Of course," Tamlin said. "I chose alchemy myself. I considered evocation for a while, but it didn't really speak to me. But we're here to learn and grow into contributing members of society and great mages one day!"

Just then, a voice called out, firm and sharp. “All right, class, eyes up front. We’ve got a new student today.”

A tall man with dark hair and piercing blue eyes stepped onto the central platform. His robes shimmered slightly when he moved, woven with strands of arcane magic.

“Emric Vale, correct?” the professor asked, turning toward him.

Emric stood and tried to look composed, giving a very stiff bow. “Yes, sir.”

Professor Beck studied him for a second. “Any relation to Liora Vale?”

Emric looked down. “Yes. She was my mother.”

A brief silence followed. Some students glanced at each other. Others sat up a bit straighter. A few whispered under their breath.

Beck, not wanting to press the wound he’d accidentally prodded, gave a slow, thoughtful nod. “Very well. Take your seat.”

Emric sat quickly, cheeks warm. He could feel eyes on him, not cruel, just curious.

Professor Beck stepped forward and waved his hand over the central platform. The runes shimmered and rearranged themselves into a three-dimensional outline of a tall spiraling tower.

"Today we'll start with a refresher on magic and its relationship to personal practice," Beck said. "Who can tell me what building this is, and why you should all care?"

Tamlin's hand shot up, but Beck gave him an expectant look to another student instead. "Madison, you haven't said anything in a while. Can you tell us what this is?"

Madison's cheeks went red; she was still staring at Emric with surprise at his announcement that Liora was his mother. Her crimson hair fell in soft waves past her shoulders, and her sharp green eyes stood out against smooth, creamy skin.

Her embarrassment faded as she focused. "Yes," she said. "That's the Spire. That's where the Arcwarden Council and the eleven Crest-holders of the Web all work."

"Correct," Beck replied. "A mage's power is never separate from their responsibility.

Whether you join a guild, enter the private sector, or serve under a Crest-holder in one of the Pillars, you remain governed by law."

Then he turned toward Emric. "Mister Vale. Can you name one of the five Pillars and describe its role?"

Emric hesitated for only a second, then cleared his throat. "The Pillar of Authority governs law enforcement: city marshals, court-mages, and magical investigation teams.

They make sure magic is used legally and that rogue mages are dealt with."

Beck gave a small, satisfied nod. “Correct,” he said, turning back to the class.

Tamlin shot Emric a quick thumbs-up.

When class ended, students gathered their things. A few glanced at Emric again. One girl in bright orange glasses walked past and muttered, “Nice save, Vale.”

Emric blinked, unsure if it was a compliment or sarcasm.

As he stood to leave, Tamlin appeared at his side. “Not bad for your first day. Don’t worry, you’ll fit right in. And if you ever want to study together or talk Spire politics, I’m a bit obsessed.”

Emric nodded, genuinely grateful. “Thanks. I might take you up on that.”

“Oh, and later this week, we’re doing domain exposure labs. You’ll get to test-drive a few schools of magic and see if anything clicks. It might help you decide.”

Emric’s stomach tensed, but he nodded anyway.

Chapter 2

The apartment door clicked open with a soft chime from the expired protective wards. Nia glanced at the runes and shrugged. "I guess Dad still hasn't refreshed them yet."

She stepped in first, kicking off her shoes and tossing her bag toward the couch. Emric followed more slowly, his eyes drifting to the dark hallway that led to their father's room.

The door was still closed, the same as when they had left that morning.

"He hasn't moved," Emric said quietly.

Nia didn't respond right away. She stood there for a moment, then sighed and walked into the kitchen. Placing her hand on the sigil next to the icebox, she opened it and peered inside. "We're out of milk," she muttered. "Again."

Before Emric could answer, the front door clicked again. Their older brother, Kael, stepped inside, wearing the sleek uniform of a mana engineer: a dark-gray coat stitched with gold thread and the faint hum of arcane tools still clinging to his belt. He was tall and broad-shouldered, carrying himself like someone who hadn't stopped moving since the day their mother died. He looked like a taller version of Emric, only with darker hair.

Kael glanced at Nia, and a small smile broke through his otherwise hard features. "Hey, kiddo. How was your first day at the new school?"

Nia lit up. "It was amazing, Kael! I'm in the advanced track, and my professor, Professor Grenlyn, says I've got a knack for fine-tuned shaping spells. Oh, and we got our mana tags today!"

Kael tousled her hair. "I'm not surprised. You've always had a sharp mind for detail." He looked at her with genuine pride.

Then his eyes slid past her and locked onto Emric. The air in the room seemed to tighten.

Kael's smile faded. "You make it to class?"

Emric nodded. "Yeah. Room 41. Professor Beck."

"Figured they'd stick you in the basics." The words weren't cruel, just sharp enough to land.

Emric's jaw tightened. "I'm still finding my direction."

Kael looked irritated. "You've been finding your direction for three years."

Nia, sensing the tension in the room, stepped in quickly. "Emric did fine. He even got called on in class and answered perfectly."

Kael said nothing. He dropped his satchel by the door, walked past his brother and sister, and paused outside their father's room.

Still closed.

Still dark.

He didn't bother knocking. He stared at the door for a heartbeat too long, then turned toward the kitchen. "I'll pick up groceries later. You two can eat whatever's left."

"Thanks, Kael," Nia said softly. Emric stayed silent.

As Kael opened the icebox and scanned the contents, he spoke again without turning around. "We're not kids anymore. The world's not waiting for us to catch up." Then, cool and pointed: "Some people already wasted their chance."

He didn't look at Emric when he said it. He didn't need to.

Emric stood frozen, his fingers twitching at his sides.

Nia shot her eldest brother a look—half hurt, half furious—but said nothing. She knew it wouldn't help.

Kael shut the icebox with a quiet thud, grabbed a mana-bar from the counter, and disappeared into his room without another word.

The silence that followed was suffocating.

Nia leaned in and quietly said, "I know he doesn't really blame you."

Emric kept his eyes on Kael's doorway. "I don't know about that."

The silence in the room settled deeper, thick enough to feel.

In his mind, Emric heard the unbidden and unwanted voice of a news anchor.

Ten Years Ago

The family sat bunched together on the couch as a voice echoed from the Aetherplate, its surface flickering with glimmers of mana.

"—incredible mana shaping under extreme pressure," the anchor's voice rang out. "Liora Vale, ranked number eight among the Ten Most Powerful Mages, was key in preventing what experts are now calling the worst necromantic outbreak in over a century here in New York."

The image shifted to bonewalkers scattering under collapsing death glyphs, fog thick with eerie deathlight rolling across shattered cobblestones.

"She personally disrupted two ritual circles mid-cast," the anchor continued, "and deployed a field-wide cascade of unbinding seals to sever the soul anchors before they could latch into the graveyard's ley line."

A new clip shimmered into view: Liora, coat singed and trailing threads of controlled flame, carving a warding sigil into stone with a glowing blade of mana.

"Eyewitnesses say she advanced through the breach alone," the anchor added, "ignoring the rising soulfire, as she called for the collapse of the eastern ley channel to cut off the necromancer's anchor array."

From the couch, Kael jumped so high he nearly hit his head on the ceiling. "Did you see that? She broke the anchor with a fire arc! Hot damn!"

"Language!" came Liora's voice from the other room—though she was clearly laughing.

Emric leaned forward, eyes wide. "Did you see that double-cast she did? She hit and reshaped the necromancers with a flamebind before they could finish their chant."

He turned, and he and Kael slapped a high five.

"Well," their father said proudly, "she is your mother, after all. Of course she can."

Nia giggled. "Mom's better than everyone!"

Liora appeared behind the couch, placing a warm hand on each of her sons' heads. Emric beamed up at her. "One day, that's going to be me right up there with you, Mom!"

"Oh, I don't doubt it," Liora said, kneeling to meet his gaze. "All three of you will. I know it."

But her eyes lingered on Emric just a second longer.

Their father reached for her hand, pulling her in gently as Nia snuggled closer on his knee.

"They're going to talk about this for a century," he said.

Liora kissed his cheek. "That's fine," she whispered. "This moment is the only one I care about."

Chapter 3

Emric woke the next morning before the sun rose.

The apartment was quiet, no footsteps or voices, only the faint hum of the floating city beyond the window. Mana trails sliding along skyrails as early commuters drifted to work.

He stared at the ceiling, waiting for the weight on his chest to lift. It never did.

His mana tag pulsed softly on the desk across the room, a blinking blue reminder:

08:00 — Domain Exposure Lab.

Emric sat up and rubbed his eyes. Day two at Cloudrest.

He'd survived day one. It had even given him a sliver of hope.

He hadn't expected his classmates to understand his decision to wait before choosing a domain.

Kael certainly didn't.

He recalled Kael's words from last night:

"You've been finding your direction for three years."

Emric scrunched his face in frustration.

It was the same thing Kael always said. But maybe… maybe he wasn't wrong.

Emric had waited because he was supposed to, because he was told to.

His mother had promised they'd pick it together—

that she'd help him find his domain and hone his skill.

But that future had been stolen.

She had been stolen.

Then the waiting turned to doubt.

The doubt to indecision.

And the indecision, finally, to silence.

Emric stood, crossed the room, and slipped his mana tag into his school bag. He pressed his hand to the wall sigil.

Light bloomed from the gloworb overhead.

He dressed in silence: gray tunic, reinforced jacket, simple boots. No frills.

No domain crest.

He didn't have one. Not yet.

But maybe that was about to change.

A note was pinned to Professor Beck's homeroom door:

Domain Exposure Lab today — Room 50, Lower Arcana Wing. Instructor: Prof. G. Moss

The Lower Arcana Wing wasn't on his map, but he went anyway. After circling past the illusions annex, across two floating walkways, and down a staircase he swore hadn't been there before, he found Room 50.

Inside the classroom, everybody was already in their seats – but Tamlin eagerly waved him over. "You found it! Honestly, I wasn't sure if you would."

"Yeah, it took me a while. This school's layout isn't as simple as you'd think it would be."

Tamlin nodded. "Don't worry, you'll get used to it. Especially with Professor Moss—his classroom is in a weird place, and that's on par for him because he's a weird guy... well, you'll see."

Emric blinked. "What?"

Tamlin was about to answer, but the sound of glass shattering cut him off. Emric turned.

At the front of the class stood what appeared to be a goat. Tall. Bipedal. Wearing a patched-up robe over a blazer with visible bite marks in the sleeves. His head was entirely goat—bearded and horned. His feet were cloven hooves. A thin tail flicked beneath the coat.

But his hands were unmistakably human.

His tail had knocked a glass jar—some sort of potion—off his desk. That was the sound that had interrupted them.

The professor spun around wide-eyed and bleated:

"BLEEAAAAH!"

A long, awkward pause followed.

Then, as if nothing had happened, he turned back to the board and continued drawing runes.

"That," Tamlin whispered, "is Professor Moss. He used to be one of the top transfiguration mages in the country. Never quite broke into the top ten rankings, but people still knew his name. Then one day he tried to prove a theory about self-transfiguration and ended up turning himself mostly into a goat."

Emric stared. "Why doesn't he just change back?"

"Officially," Tamlin said, "he says he's still gathering data on the spell. But unofficially, a group of us think he can't figure out how to reverse it—and he's too proud to admit it."

"So he's stuck like that?"

Tamlin grinned. "I think so. Even if he won't admit it."

Once Moss finished drawing his runes, he turned to the class.

"Welcome to today's Domain Exposure Lab, where you'll learn to identify the magical discipline best suited to your soul signature—or at the very least the one you won't accidentally explode while using.

"And for those of you who have already picked a domain," he added, "you will be of great help to the ones who are still undecided."

He began to pace, hooves clacking and tail swishing. He gestured toward the glowing runes behind him.

"Most of you already know the eleven domains recognized by the Spire," Moss said. "But let's humor the educational process, shall we?"

"BLEEAAAAH!"

He pointed at Tamlin. "Tamlin, stand up!"

Tamlin jumped to his feet, hands at his sides.

"Mr. Peer Leader, enlighten your classmates. Name the eleven domains recognized by the Spire."

"Of course, Professor."

Tamlin cleared his throat, blushing. "There's the Crest of Elements, Iron, Chain… uh…" He trailed off, blanking.

Professor Moss blinked both goat eyes at him. "Astounding. I shall treasure that contribution always."

He turned to another student. "Miss… Nightfall, isn't it?"

Madison nodded. "Yes, professor."

"Save us, won't you? BLEEAAAAH!"

She stood and said, "Elements, Iron, Chain, Wards, Veil, Mind, Sight, Essence, Bloom, Surge, and Arcane."

Professor Moss stomped his hoof in approval. "Thank you, Miss Nightfall. A mind like a steel trap."

He turned back to the board and began connecting the runes in the shape of a web.

"This is why we call them the Web. They all affect one another. Some domains have more influence on their neighbors than others, but every domain ripples through the rest."

"Each spell you cast, every scroll you buy, every tome you read—it can all be traced to one of these crests. Which is why picking your domain is such a vital part of your magical development."

He paused, then added, "Even if you pick the Crest of Elements and specialize in elemental magic, you can still use spells from the Crest of Wards. But your strength in that domain will always be less than someone trained in it directly."

Moss clacked his hoof and raised his hand dramatically.

"However..."

Outside the web, another crest appeared, floating and unattached. "If this web is so complete, why does it feel like something is missing?" His tail gave a small but noticeable twitch.

Emric leaned forward, curious about what the professor was getting at. Moss closed his eyes and took a deep breath. Then:

“Tell me, students, has it ever occurred to you that perhaps—just perhaps—the Spire is hiding something?”

The room fell completely silent.

Emric glanced at Tamlin, who mouthed, “Here we go.”

Professor Moss began pacing again, his hooves clicking out a rhythm of rising excitement, his tail twitching as he walked.

“The Spire teaches that the web is complete—eleven domains, each balanced with its two adjacent domains. But I believe that is utter hooey!”

“BLEEAAAAH!”

“Any mage who casts outside their own crest knows the web pulls in strange directions.

There are…” Moss trailed off as if searching for the right word, “resonances—empty spaces where something should be!”

He pointed at the unattached rune hovering outside the diagram, voice rising with enthusiasm.

“This! Right here. This is the missing piece. No official documentation. No sanctioned curriculum. But the pull from the magic is there!”

He was about to continue when Professor Beck’s voice called from the back of the room—tired, more annoyed than angry.

“Moss, not this again.”

Moss froze mid–tail swish. His ears perked up, and he let out a tiny, “bleeaah.”

Beck stepped into full view, his arms crossed, expression weary. “Just stick to the curriculum.”

“Very well,” Moss replied in a defeated tone.

Moss waved his hand, and the twelfth crest vanished. The floating diagram once again showed only eleven crests.

“Back to the boring version.”

Professor Moss clapped his hands together twice to get the attention of the students who had spaced out during his theory on the Twelfth Crest.

“All right, enough with the lecture. Time for practical application!” he announced.

“Professor Beck has told me we have a higher-than-average number of students who haven’t chosen their domains yet, so we’re breaking into groups of three: two students who’ve already chosen their domains and one who has not.

“If you’ve chosen your Crest—congratulations. You now have teaching responsibilities.”

With a flick of his wrist, shimmering glyphs spun through the air. Emric’s mana tag pulsed in response and began to glow green.

Around the room, students began moving—rearranging themselves, shifting chairs, and shuffling backpacks as groups slowly began to form based on color.

Moss called their attention to a floating diagram showing that Green Group would be:

Tamlin Ethington, Madison Nightfall, and Emric Vale.

Tamlin was already grinning and waving him over. Madison raised an eyebrow and gave a little chin-nod toward the empty seat beside her.

He took it.

"I guess we're stuck with each other," Tamlin said cheerfully, plopping down across from Emric. "Not that I'm complaining."

Madison looked up from the notes she was taking, a bit unsure of herself, then added, "Just as long as you don't melt anything this time."

"Nobody got hurt," Tamlin replied with a shrug.

Madison raised an eyebrow. "You melted a cauldron."

"I upgraded a cauldron."

Emric blinked and shook his head to regain composure. "So… what Crest did you choose?"

Tamlin straightened like a banner catching the wind. "Crest of Iron—specifically in mana chemistry. Potions are my specialty. I've been experimenting with multi-stage infusions and elementally reactive brews. I made one last month that turns your skin into a rock-like material."

Madison's eyebrows lifted in surprise. Emric turned to her. "What about you?"

She smiled, a little shyly. "Crest of Mind. I specialize in enchantment—taking something mundane and weaving threads of mana through it to give it magical properties."

She glanced at him, her voice softening. "Since Tamlin and I already have our crests, that must mean you haven't picked one yet?"

"That's okay, though," she said quickly, realizing how that might've come across. "That's what this lab is for. We compare the different domains and see which ones resonate with you. It's kind of like magical speed dating."

She turned bright red as soon as she said dating, eyes flicking away from Emric.

Tamlin, completely oblivious, leaned forward. "We just ran through a few crest-aligned spells by reading some scrolls. See what you like best—or what pulls at you. Sometimes it's subtle, sometimes it hits like a punch to the chest."

Professor Moss began moving around the room, handing out small bundles of scrolls to each group.

"I'm giving each group eleven scrolls," he said, then muttered under his breath, "Should be twelve…"

He raised his voice again. “Remember, be careful with each scroll. Unlike tomes, once you read it, the spell is used up and can’t be re-read. These are not toys, and I do not have an unlimited stockpile.”

Emric turned to Madison. “How did you pick your Crest, Madison?”

“Madi!” she said quickly, then softened. “Sorry—I mean, please call me Madi. I don’t like Madison.”

There was a moment—just a heartbeat—where her eyes met his and lingered. Her cheeks flushed again, and she quickly looked over at the scrolls Professor Moss had just given their group.

“We should probably get started on the scrolls. We don’t want to waste them,” she said, trying to change the subject.

Tamlin perked up. “Yes! The scrolls! This is the best part.”

He reached out and carefully spread the bundle across the table. Each one was rolled tight and bound with color-coded thread—red for Elements, green for Bloom, violet for Mind, and so on.

Emric leaned forward, scanning the scrolls.

So many paths.So many directions.

How was he supposed to choose?

He reached for the red-threaded scroll: Elements.

He didn't grab it immediately. He just let his fingers hover near it, hesitating.

It was the Crest his mother, Liora, had worn. He'd seen it etched on her clothing from the time he was born, glowing when her magic was activated. It was the domain of elemental power, where the elements bent and flowed to her will.

He wanted that. He still wanted to be just like her.

Even if he wasn't sure he deserved it.

He picked up the scroll, trying not to show how tightly he was gripping it.

"Starting with the Elements?" Tamlin asked, leaning forward with curiosity. "Solid choice. Classic!"

Emric shrugged, trying to play it off. "Figured I'd start simple."

He didn't mention the real reason; he just took a deep breath and unfurled the scroll.

The scroll crackled faintly with dormant energy as Emric unrolled it. Neatly written in elegant script was a basic firebolt incantation—simple, controlled, and meant for first years.

"It won't activate unless you intend to cast it," Tamlin said, watching closely. "You can read it and study the runes without triggering the effect."

Emric nodded and ran his fingers gently over the symbols. The mana woven through the parchment glowed a faint red along the edges. The letters were clean and easy to read—he had learned spellform in elementary school, like all children, long before they were ever allowed to cast.

He studied the casting sequence, visualized the runes in motion, and let the incantation settle in his mind. He raised his hand, aimed at one of the practice dummies lined against the far wall, and spoke the final command aloud.

The scroll flared and vanished in a puff of fire.

The magic surged through his arm—a pull, a thread weaving from his center outward in a web, just as Professor Moss had described. He felt the fire take form: heat rushing to his fingertips, the spell coalescing in an instant.

A firebolt rocketed out of his hand and struck the target square in the chest. A clean hit.

Controlled.

Effective.

The dummy smoked slightly. A faint ripple of heat shimmered in the air along the firebolt's path.

Tamlin let out a low whistle. "Nice shot!"

Madi blinked, impressed. "Why haven't you picked a Crest yet? That clearly wasn't your first time casting."

Emric stood there, his expression unreadable.

He'd hit the target perfectly. He'd done everything right.

So why did it feel... wrong?

The pull of the web had been there. He'd felt it clearly—the tug of mana aligning through the Web like a current guiding his hand. But it was shallow, like striking the right note on an instrument you didn't really know how to play.

It worked.

But it didn't fit.

He wanted this; he had never wanted anything else in the world this badly. To be like his mother. But deep down, a quiet voice was already whispering.

"This isn't yours."

He pulled his hand back and looked down at his fingertips, and said nothing.

Emric exhaled slowly, forcing his expression to relax.

"That was cool," he said, trying to sound casual. "But the only way I can describe it is... it's not me."

Tamlin didn't miss a beat. "All right! On to the next one."

He shuffled the scrolls like a kid opening birthday presents. "Let's try Iron next—you're gonna love this one, I promise! It's got structure. It's got force. It's my personal choice!"

Emric took the scroll with the metallic gray threading and unfurled the Crest of Iron.

This one wasn't offensive magic—it was a simple transmutation spell designed to turn a rock into a hunk of glass.

He read the script, focused, and cast. The result was… fine.

Another clear tug through the Web, another clean spell cast. But again, he heard the whisper inside him: This isn't yours.

"Well?" Tamlin asked, still eager.

"Sorry. I don't think this one is for me either," Emric responded.

A bit disheveled, Tamlin nodded but kept his enthusiasm up. Next came the Crest of Mind.

As Emric picked up the scroll, he noticed Madi watching him, her fingertips curled nervously around the edge of the table. She wasn't smiling—just holding her breath.

The scroll was wrapped in violet thread. The script was sharper, more elegant. The spell contained within was a basic focus charm, a clarity boost meant to sharpen perception.

He cast.

The spell wrapped around his mind like a thin layer of ice—sharp, sterile, cold. His awareness expanded, details sharpening, but it felt like he was wearing someone else's glasses.

When the effect faded, he shook his head. "Nope."

Madi's face fell slightly. She looked away, cheeks coloring. "It's… not for everyone," she said, trying to brush it off.

Scroll by scroll, Emric kept testing.

Chain. Wards. Veil. Sight. Surge. Essence.

Each spell worked. Some were clunky, others surprisingly smooth. But none of them fit.

He only had two scrolls left—Arcane and Bloom. Emric reached for the next one: the Crest of Arcane.

The moment his fingers touched the scroll, something inside him lit up.

Warmth swelled in his chest—not the heat of a flame, but something deeper, like a light switching on in a part of himself he hadn't realized was dark.

And then—

You have more power than you know.

The voice wasn't external. It came from within, the same one that had whispered to him earlier.

But this time it wasn't doubt.

It wasn't resistance. It was recognition.

The scroll hadn't even activated yet. He hadn't spoken the command. He didn't need to.

It was already speaking to him.

He took a slow breath, trying to contain his excitement, and unfurled the scroll. The ink shimmered in shifting lines of deep blue—clean, structured, powerful. Arcane magic.

Raw spellcraft. The framework behind every other domain.

He read the incantation aloud.

The scroll flared to life, bursting into sparks of blue-violet light that swirled around his fingertips.

This time, the magic didn't tug through the Web.

It flowed.

It wasn't just a light switching on in a dark room.

It was like stepping through a doorway into a place he had been searching for all his life without realizing it.

The same voice whispered again:

This is what your mother had planned for you.

And he knew.

She would have wanted him to choose this.

He had always thought she would guide him into the Crest of Elements—that she would be there, steady and sure, leading him forward until he was ready.

But he'd been wrong.

She would have directed him here.

Not because it was hers—but because it was his.

He raised his hand.

No hesitation. No doubt.

The magic shimmered at his fingertips, arcing in elegant strands. And then—

A bolt of raw magical energy, a magic missile, streaked from his fingers—bright, fast, precise.

It struck the center of the target dummy and exploded in a controlled burst of violet-white light.

The entire class turned to look.

The dummy—or rather, what was left of it—was a blackened, scorched husk. The air buzzed faintly, like static in the silence after a thunderclap.

Emric exhaled, lowered his hand, and just smiled.

Chapter 4

The apartment door slid open with a soft chime.

Nia burst inside before it even finished, practically skipping over the threshold. "I am so happy for you, Emric!" she said, dropping her bag on the freshly cleaned rug. "This is so exciting!"

Emric followed close behind, his gaze drifting to the darkened hallway.

The door to their father's room was still shut.

Same as this morning. Same as yesterday. Same as the day before that.

Nia didn't comment. She peeled off her shoes and beelined for the kitchen. A second later, she let out an excited shout.

"Yay, Kael went grocery shopping!"

She bounded back in, clutching a big bowl of moondrops—a glittering, gumdrop-like candy that glowed faintly in the dark.

"He knows me so well," she said, popping one into her mouth.

Kael's voice carried from his room. "Don't eat the candy. I'm about to make dinner."

"Too late!" Nia giggled.

Kael emerged, gave her a loving shake of his head, and smiled like it couldn't be helped.

The living room was almost unrecognizable—the moving boxes were gone, the bookshelf half-stacked, framed photos already on the walls. Kael worked fast when he wanted to.

"Whatcha gonna make?" Nia beamed, practically dancing over. She was too excited to care about dinner. "Hey! Guess what?"

Kael's eyes flicked to Emric's shoulder—the school bag still slung there, a fresh thread of silver embroidery stitched into the strap.

The Crest of Arcane.

Kael's jaw tightened.

He tried to relax his face but couldn't quite manage it as he turned back to Nia.

"I don't know," he said flatly. "What?"

Nia rolled her eyes, oblivious. "Emric picked a crest! And not just that—he destroyed one of the target dummies in Professor Moss's class today. Like, blew it to bits. Professor Moss was all excited about it, and he made a bunch of weird goat noises."

Kael looked at her, brow furrowed. "Goat noises?"

Nia waved a hand. "It's complicated. I'll fill you in later. He's like a half-man, half-goat thing. Actually, that's it. I don't need to fill you in—you get it now."

Emric shifted awkwardly in the doorway.

Kael didn't look at him at first.

Then, without a glimmer of approval, he muttered, "It's about damn time."

Dinner was quiet at first.

Nia sat at the table, her bowl of moondrops off to the side like a secret pet she fed when no one was looking. Emric picked at the rice and stir-fried vegetables on his plate, not really hungry. Kael sat across from him, arms tense, fork scraping against the porcelain.

The silence, which felt like an eternity, was really only a few seconds.

"So…" Kael began, not looking up. "Why Arcane?"

Emric blinked. "What?"

Kael stabbed a piece of broccoli. "Your crest. You chose Arcane." His voice was calm but sharp around the edges. "Not Elements."

The question hung in the air like smoke.

Kael continued, "Everyone thought Mommy's little boy would've followed in her footsteps."

Emric's fingers tightened around his fork.

"Kael..." Nia said softly, worried that another yelling session would break out.

But Kael paid her no mind.

"I mean, that's what everyone expected of you, right?" Kael's tone was bitter now, low and biting. "She always said you were the one who had the spark. Not me."

Emric looked quietly confused.

"Kael, stop," Nia said, firmer this time. She looked between the two of them, clearly not new to this particular fight. "Can we just not do this tonight?"

Kael didn't answer. He leaned back in his chair, arms crossed, still glaring at Emric.

Nia rushed to change the subject. "Anyway! My class started Advanced Divination today!" she said with forced brightness. "Professor Grenlyn said I already have one of the sharpest Sight alignments he's ever seen. He gave me this enchanted notebook that auto-records visions and everything—"

"Did you get any tomes yet?" Kael cut in, eyes still focused on Emric.

That threw Emric for a second. The edge was still there in Kael's voice, but something else had slipped in too.

Curiosity, maybe.

Emric shook his head. "No. I haven't had a chance to go to the shops yet."

Kael narrowed his eyes. "You haven't even read your starter tome?"

"I haven't had a chance since coming home, and I wanted to see if they had anything else I could use at the shop. I haven't even found my fluxbag yet—it's still packed away in one of the moving boxes."

Kael let out a sharp, annoyed breath.

"I found your fluxbag," he said, pushing back from the table. "I put it on your bed earlier while I was unpacking."

"Oh. Thank you," Emric said softly but gratefully.

"Try checking your room next time before declaring a treasure hunt," Kael muttered. "You want to be a mage? Start acting like one." He left the kitchen without looking back.

Emric lowered his gaze to his plate. "Thanks... for that too," he mumbled.

Later that night, Emric sat cross-legged on his bed, a tangle of cords and books still surrounding him from unpacked boxes. His fluxbag sat on his nightstand, right where Kael had said he'd left it. He hadn't opened it yet.

Instead, he powered up his aetherplate that hung on his wall, the faint blue glow of its crystal core flickering to life inside the casing. The screen shimmered, projecting a floating interface in front of him.

Messages. Updates. System pings.

One unread notification blinked in the corner: "Message from: MILES."

Emric's face broke into a grin.

He tapped the message. It opened:

"Hey man, how's it going? Are you unpacked yet? We sure miss you over here. Give me your new mana tag info when you get it so we can connect. Later."

Emric smiled to himself and let out a soft laugh. He sent his new mana tag information to Miles.

A couple of seconds later, his aetherplate began to pulse gently around the edges.

Incoming call: Miles Thorne.

Emric answered.

A kid about his age appeared on screen—dark-skinned, gum-chewing—always gum-chewing—and grinning like he didn't have a care in the world. His hair was a mess in that perfectly calculated way, like he'd spent forty minutes trying to look like he hadn't spent any time on it at all. He had that same easygoing energy that made it seem like nothing ever rattled him.

Miles had been Emric's best friend since before either of them could walk. Loyal, sharp, and a little too smart for his own good, he was one of the only people Emric could truly be himself around.

"Yo!" Miles grinned, a mouth full of gum. "Took you long enough to call me back. I sent that message to you yesterday."

"You know," Emric said, "getting settled. I haven't even unpacked my room yet."

He reached up and spun the aetherial screen floating in the air, turning it toward his room to show Miles the still-packed boxes, then spun it back to face himself.

"Good luck with that, man," Miles said, settling back in his chair. "So, how's floating around in Utah? Any snowstorms yet?"

"Nah, but I hear they're coming soon," Emric replied. "Still getting adjusted. Everything feels like it's in the wrong place."

"Yeah," Miles said with a crooked smile, "including you. Wanna play a quick game of StarCraft?"

Emric raised an eyebrow. "Quick? I don't think that's possible. With the way you overanalyze things, the quickest game of StarCraft you could manage is about a week long."

Miles burst out laughing, nearly choking on his gum. "Okay, rude, but fair."

They both laughed for a minute. Emric felt normal again—like New York hadn't been replaced by floating cities and a giant mountain range.

They started the game and picked their races. Once it loaded, Miles asked casually, like a joke,

"So... you finally pick a crest yet, or are you gonna be the only uncrested mage at your graduation?"

Emric paused—just long enough to make it real.

"Yeah," he said. "I did."

Miles blinked. "Wait. What?"

"I picked one," Emric repeated, almost sheepishly.

Miles leaned forward into the screen, eyes wide. "You're messing with me."

"Nope."

"You're serious?"

Emric nodded.

Miles stared, gum forgotten for a second—which was saying a lot. "What'd you pick?"

"Arcane."

Dead silence.

Miles blinked once. Twice.

"Are you kidding me?"

Miles threw his hands up. “Arcane?! You picked Arcane?!”

Emric scratched the back of his head. “Yeah. It just kind of clicked.”

“Dude.” Miles leaned even closer into the screen. “You have no idea how jealous I am right now. That was my dream Crest! Back when we were ten, I had a whole notebook full of Arcane spells, theories, and combos. Do you remember that?”

Emric laughed. “Yeah, I do.”

“Yeah!” Miles shot back. “I even had cool names for them!”

Emric raised an eyebrow.

Miles held up his hands. “Fine. I had some cool names for them. But still! I was obsessed with Arcane.”

“Then why didn’t you pick it?” Emric asked.

Miles paused, gum rolling between his teeth. “I tried. A bunch of times. But it never... felt right. Like it was close, but not mine, you know?”

Emric nodded. He could very much relate to that feeling—especially after today.

Miles shrugged. “Then Surge hit me like a lightning bolt. Once I was able to harness that energy—oh man, I never looked back.”

Emric smiled. “Yeah. Surge does fit you.”

“Sure,” Miles said. “It’s not bad. I’ve got some kinetic stuff that’s pretty sick. But Arcane, man—that Crest is pure potential. It’s like raw possibility that you can shape into anything.”

The boys were so into talking that neither of them noticed their bases on the screen being ransacked by zerglings, hydralisks, and mutalisks.

Miles finally sat back down and said, “Okay, okay, I’ve got a couple of spells you have to try once you get the chance. I hope your shops have them like they do here. In fact, what kind of spells do they even have over there?”

Emric shrugged. “I don’t know. I haven’t been shopping yet.”

“Okay, well if they have them,” Miles continued without missing a beat, “there’s one called *Mirror Lance* and another called *Phase Bolt Loop*. That one’s difficult, but if you’re as good as I know you are, you’ll get it—no problem.”

“You really think so?”

“Emric,” Miles said, suddenly serious, “I’ve seen what you can do when you stop doubting yourself. You didn’t just pick Arcane—Arcane picked you too. And I guarantee you’re gonna do things with it that no one’s even thought of yet.”

Emric didn’t say anything right away.

Then the boys suddenly realized what was happening in their game and gave their full attention to the Terran and Protoss armies currently being shredded into oblivion.

Chapter 5

The rune flickered beneath Emric's finger, glowing faintly red along the curling edge of the parchment. He bit his lip and tried again, carefully dragging his fingertip along the mana-ink. The spellform shimmered for a second—an almost-perfect Lava Burst glyph—before sputtering out with a soft fizz.

Still too fast.

He shifted on the floor, adjusting the pillow beneath his knees. The living room was dim, lit by a single gloworb floating in the corner. Around him, scrolls and spellform primers were scattered like petals in a ritual circle.

In the next room, the voices of his parents drifted gently through the air—too soft for Emric to catch the words, but clear enough to know who was speaking.

"He's been at it all evening," Liora said, the smile in her voice unmistakable. "Tracing the same scroll until his fingers cramp—he won't stop until he gets it perfect."

"Sounds like someone else I know."

"I never had that kind of discipline at his age," she laughed softly.

There was a pause.

"Are you worried about him?"

"Not at all," she said. "I'm... amazed. I love all our children, Darian. I love all three of them with my whole soul. But Emric..."

She hesitated, her voice dropping to a near whisper. "There's something in him I don't see in Kael or Nia—a kind of spark. I don't know how to explain it. Like the magic already knows him."

Kael sat motionless on the stairs, hidden in the shadowed hallway, knees pulled to his chest, heart thudding. He hadn't meant to eavesdrop—he just hadn't wanted to go upstairs yet. Now he didn't want to move at all.

"Kael's strong," Darian said. "And Nia's brilliant."

"They are," Liora agreed. "They're both going to do amazing things. But Emric... there's something deeper in him. He feels magic in a way I've never seen before."

Liora reached over and rested her head on Darian's shoulder. There was quiet for a moment before Darian spoke again, voice low.

"You know I'd give everything to keep you safe, right?"

"I know."

"Even if the world needed saving, and it meant losing you—"

"Shh," she whispered. "Don't talk like that. We still have so much left to do."

Kael couldn't breathe. He hugged his knees tighter.

The couch creaked as Darian stood.

"I'll head up," he said with a yawn. "I've got to be at the hospital early."

Kael heard his father's footsteps approaching and panicked. He scrambled into bed and pretended to be asleep just as Darian passed down the hallway.

Liora's footsteps turned the other way—into the living room.

Emric didn't notice her until she knelt behind him and slipped her arms around his shoulders, pulling him into a warm hug.

"Still awake, Merlin?" she said, ruffling his hair. "At this rate, you'll be the next name in the history books."

"Almost got it," Emric mumbled, pointing at a scroll.

She smiled against his cheek. "That poor scroll's going to burn out before you do."

He turned toward her, eyes bright with determination.

"I just want to be ready, Mom. When I pick the Crest of Elements... I want to be the best. Just like you."

Her smile softened, pride and love shining in her eyes.

"Don't lock yourself into your pick too soon, sweetheart," she said gently. "You might be meant for something else."

"No chance," Emric said, shaking his head. "It'll be Elements for sure."

Liora laughed and pulled him tighter.

"Then you'd better get some sleep. Being the best takes a lot of work."

Emric blinked as sunlight spilled across the walkways of the ground district in Salt Lake City. He and Nia moved with the flow of weekend foot traffic. Colorful shop banners flapped in the breeze, glowing sigils advertising everything from rune ink to chocolate ice cream.

Nia spun around on her heel to face him, walking backward with a grin.

"So, how does it feel to finally be a crestbearer?"

Emric shrugged, trying to play it off like it wasn't a big deal, but a smile crept across his face.

"Weird. Good mostly, though. I'm still getting used to it."

"Oh, you will," she said, tossing her ponytail. "Come on. First stop—it's called *Whispering Pages.* I heard it's the best shop for beginner scrolls and tomes."

She took the lead, weaving past a merchant floating on a levitating carpet piled high with baked goods.

Just before they entered the shop, a familiar voice called through the crowd:

"Emric? Hey!"

Emric turned to see Tamlin, practically bouncing down the street, flanked by a tall young man with broad shoulders and a warm smile, and an older man in a wheelchair. The chair was being pushed by another man who looked almost identical to Tamlin, only a few years older.

Tamlin waved enthusiastically, as if he hadn't seen Emric in years. "Didn't expect to run into you here! What are you up to?"

"Scroll shopping," Nia said brightly. "Emric needs to stock up now that he's finally chosen a domain."

She leaned toward Emric and said, loud enough for Tamlin to hear, "So who's your handsome friend?"

Emric rolled his eyes at his younger sister and then gestured to Tamlin. "This is Tamlin. He's in my class—the peer leader."

Tamlin cocked his head proudly. "It is a pleasure to meet you," he said enthusiastically and shook Nia's hand. "What might your name be?"

Nia giggled a little and said, "Nia. I'm his sister."

"It's a pleasure to meet you, Nia." Then he turned and gestured to his companions. "This is my older brother, Owen. He works at the Spire doing spellcrafting. And this is my father."

The man in the wheelchair gave a polite nod. "Nice to meet you both. Heard Tamlin talk about you already, young man."

Tamlin grinned. "Only good things, I promise!"

As the introductions faded, Tamlin asked, “So, what kind of stuff are you looking for? Blasty spells? Utility glyphs? Enchanted scrolls?”

Emric blinked. “I... don’t know yet.”

“Great! That means we can find everything. I’m coming with you.”

Tamlin didn’t wait for a reply. He spun on his heel and waved them into the shop.

When the door closed, Tamlin said goodbye to Owen and their father, then rejoined Emric and Nia inside.

The shop was cramped but cozy—rows of floating shelves rotated slowly overhead, and a spiral staircase wound up to a second floor filled with tomes. Scroll tubes lined the walls, sorted neatly by domain.

Tamlin grabbed a scroll at random and unrolled it.

“Ooh, this one’s for summoning floating daggers. Kinda flashy, but not bad in a pinch.”

He handed it to Emric, who examined it with cautious interest.

“You really know your stuff,” Nia said, hopping up to reach a tome labeled *Arcane Pattern Theory.*

“Of course,” Tamlin said enthusiastically. “Crest of Iron, remember? People think it’s just potions, but it’s much more than that. Alchemy, sure, but also transmutation, structural crafting, even architectural magic."

He waved his arms for emphasis.

"Anything you can make with magic? That's the Crest of Iron. I chose potions because I like being able to throw people off and surprise them when they least expect it. But I could have gone into golem-making or forging if I wanted."

Emric raised an eyebrow. "I didn't realize the domains were that broad."

Tamlin nodded. "Most people don't. But that's why you've got to specialize in what you want. Your domain is just a door—it's up to you to figure out where it leads."

Emric looked down at the scroll in his hands. Arcane magic. Raw force, theoretical spells, unpredictable energy.

What could he do with it? He'd need to figure that out.

As they drifted through the shop, Emric collected a few scrolls and tomes—mostly beginner-level combat spells, with names like *Mana Bolt, Crackle Loop*, and *Phase Dart*. He even found *Mirror Lance* and *Phase Bolt Loop*—the ones Miles had mentioned—but they were way out of his price range.

He browsed a few non-magical books as well, one titled Rune Compression Theory, though the math inside gave him a headache after just glancing at it.

Noticing Emric's focus on combat spells, Tamlin glanced around to make sure no one was within earshot.

"Hey. Don't tell anyone I said this, but..."

He leaned closer, eyes gleaming with excitement.

"There's going to be a school-wide tournament. It hasn't been officially announced yet—they're saving it for the assembly at the beginning of the week—but as peer leader, I get early info on these things."

Nia perked up. "A tournament?"

"Yep. Teams of five. Magic duels, obstacle courses, that kind of thing. The top team gets a commendation from the Spire. And..."

He turned squarely to face Emric. "I'm putting together my own team. I've got a few teammates lined up, but I still need someone who can deal serious damage. If I'm reading it right, you're focusing your Crest on offensive magic?"

Emric blinked.

"You want me to be on your team?"

Tamlin grinned. "You've got Arcane. That's raw potential, my friend. If you're planning to specialize in offense... you're exactly what I need."

Nia stared at Emric, eyes wide with excitement, practically vibrating.

Emric looked down at the scrolls and tomes in his arms—a dozen paths, a dozen possibilities. His heart beat faster. To his surprise, it wasn't nerves he felt.

It was excitement.

He smiled.

"Yes, I'm in."

Nia squealed and started jumping up and down beside him.

For the first time in a long time, Emric felt like he wasn't just catching up.

Chapter 6

A faint shimmer of light flickered in the air before Kael, forming the beginnings of what looked like a floating, oversized toy mallet—but it was already warping out of shape.

With a frustrated grunt, Kael released the spell, and the construct dissolved in a cloud of glittering sparks.

"This is stupid," Kael muttered. "I can't get it right."

"You're thinking too hard," Darian said gently. He crouched beside his son, brushing a few glimmering remnants off Kael's sleeve. "Creation magic is as much imagination as it is control. You have to see it first."

Kael, ten years old and scowling, kicked at the grass.

On the wooden porch steps sat Emric, legs dangling, watching with wide-eyed curiosity. Nia was curled up beside him, hugging a stuffed animal and resting her chin on her knees.

They had both drifted away from their homework and storybooks, drawn outside to watch their big brother practice with his newly acquired Crest.

Darian noticed Kael's crest sitting beside his backpack instead of pinned to his chest.

"How come you're not wearing your Crest?"

Kael crossed his arms. “I don’t want to wear it yet.”

Darian tilted his head. “Why not?”

Kael didn’t answer right away. His eyes flicked to the silver pin near his backpack—the Crest of Iron, shaped like an anvil ringed with radiant lines.

“I haven’t done anything to deserve it yet,” Kael said quietly. “I haven’t even made a single magical construct.”

Darian’s gaze softened with patient love. He thought for a moment, then said,

“The Crest isn’t something you wear because you’ve proven yourself. You wear it to help you become who you’re meant to be.”

Kael glanced sideways.

“It’s not just a decoration,” Darian continued. “The crest bears a sigil that amplifies your control over your magical domain. Your Crest of Iron will help you create more stable constructs than you could on your own. It lets your mana flow in a way that matches the domain you’re naturally attuned to.”

Kael frowned. “But what if my ideas aren’t good enough?”

Darian chuckled softly. “They don’t have to be. You’re ten—not an Archmage. You’ll learn. What matters is that you try.”

A small smile tugged at the corner of Kael’s mouth.

"That's my boy," Darian said warmly.

On the porch, Emric and Nia sat in rapt attention. Emric leaned forward with sparkling eyes, and Nia gasped softly, hugging her stuffed animal tighter.

"All right," Kael said. "I'll try again."

He bent down, picked up his Crest, and pinned it to his chest. The moment it clicked into place, a soft pulse of magic rippled through the air.

Emric held his breath. Nia grabbed his arm, eyes wide.

Kael stepped back, took a breath, and focused.

A translucent mallet of mana began to form in the air again—far more solid than before.

Darian smiled. "There we go."

The flickering blue glow of the mana-infused screen lit Emric's face as he leaned forward, eyes narrowed, fingers flying across his keyboard.

"Gank mid! Gank mid!" Miles shouted through the screen. "Nunu ganks are so vicious, man. You can't stop the snowball!"

Emric laughed. "Meh, I prefer Shaco. His stealth is too good—get behind them and they're just gonna die."

They focused on their game in silence for a while, both locked in concentration. Then Emric broke it.

"I meant to tell you earlier—I got invited to join a team for a school-wide tournament. And I said yes."

On screen, Miles's eyes went huge.

"WHAT?! Bro!"

Emric laughed.

"Okay, okay—back up. What kind of tournament is this? Combat? Puzzles? Trivia quiz?"

"Honestly?" Emric said, grinning a little. "I have no clue. The guy who invited me—Tamlin—said they haven't officially announced it yet. But they will at the next school assembly."

"Well, I don't care what it is," Miles said. "You're on a team, man. That's huge. People are finally going to see what you can actually do.

"I guess," Emric said, rubbing the back of his neck. "I mean, I only just started with Arcane. I don't even have strong spells yet."

"Did you at least pick up Mirror Lance or Phase Bolt Loop?"

"I saw them," Emric said, "but I didn't have enough for either of those tomes. They must be super strong."

"I get that," Miles groaned. "I didn't think they'd be that pricey—but yeah, they're strong, so it makes sense."

"Yeah," Emric said. "But I did get a few tomes I'm excited about. I got Arcane Blast, Arcane Explosion, and I splurged the last of my orbs on a kind of expensive spell—but awesome—*Polymorph.*"

Miles gasped.

"*Polymorph*?! No way. That's such a troll spell. I love it!"

"Yeah," Emric said with a grin. "Mine turns the target into a tiny koala bear. For like, five seconds, I think."

"Yes! Total chaos spell. You need to promise me you'll use it in the tournament."

"I make no promises. I don't even know what we're going to be doing."

Miles laughed. "Man, I wish I could be there. We'd be vicious together on the same team. That's okay, though. You'd better give me live updates—I'm so hyped for you, bro."

"I'll do my best," Emric said.

The game ended. The enemy nexus exploded in a burst of light.

Emric yawned.

"That's enough for me tonight, man. I'll talk to you later."

"Sounds good. Later, man."

Emric was just about to climb into bed when he realized his stomach was growling.

He stood there for a minute, debating whether he was more tired or hungrier.

In the end, hunger won.

He padded into the kitchen, the quiet hum of the Icebox filling the silent house. Placing his hand on the glowing sigil, he watched as the door swung open with a lazy hiss.

He grabbed a couple of sticks of string cheese, debating grabbing a Mountain Dew too—but if he had caffeine now, sleep would never happen. With a resigned sigh, he reached for a cup instead and turned toward the sink.

He was just about to fill it when his father walked in.

Startled, Emric spoke softly. “I didn’t mean to wake you.”

“You didn’t,” his father replied. “Couldn’t sleep.”

Darian sat down at the table while Emric filled two glasses of water. He brought one over and set it gently in front of his father before sitting across from him.

For a moment, neither of them said anything.

Then Darian spoke.

“Kael told me you picked your Crest.”

Emric nodded.

Darian’s gaze softened. His voice cracked, just slightly.

“Your mother would’ve been proud too... I just wish she could’ve seen it.”

He looked at Emric and added, "I'm proud of you. Truly. I know how long you waited."

Emric stared at the water in his glass, watching the ripples still.

"She used to talk about you," Darian went on, his voice distant, like he was looking through time. "Said you had something special. She called it a spark. Said it was like magic already knew you—like it was just waiting for you to catch up."

A spark.

Emric blinked. Kael had said the same thing the other night...

But Mom had never said it to him. Not once.

She must have told Dad and Kael, he thought.

Darian paused, then added quietly,

"She loved all you kids. Loved you more than I've ever seen anyone love anything. Kael's determination, Nia's brilliance... it kills me that she's missing you grow up."

There was a long pause.

"You know she—"

"She's gone, Dad," Emric said, cutting him off gently. "She's gone."

His father looked stunned.

Emric kept his voice calm—not accusatory, not angry. Just honest.

"Look... I know it's hard. It was hard on all of us. And yeah, you're still here, but... you're not. Not really. You're missing us grow up too."

He took a breath.

"I miss you. Kael misses you. Nia misses you. Mom has an excuse. What's your excuse?"

The silence that followed was heavy and absolute. Even the hum of the Icebox felt distant.

After a long while, Darian finally looked up.

"Goodnight, son," he said.

He stood, reached for the glass Emric had set out for him, and carried it with him as he walked to his room—leaving Emric alone at the kitchen table.

Chapter 7

The wind was quiet up here, like the city itself had turned the volume down. The floating training terrace Emric found sat tucked in a quiet corner of Sugar House Park. It was a cozy little spot the city had designated for public spell practice, complete with a dampening field to soften the impact of stray blasts. A soft hum lingered in the air, like the place was awake but still lounging in bed—alive, but not ready to rise.

This kind of quiet is exactly what I needed.

Emric stood at the center of a circular platform, breathing evenly. A rune circle was etched neatly into the stone beneath his feet—one of many safeguards to keep everyday magic from spiraling out of control in public zones like this.

"Okay," he whispered to himself. "Again."

He lifted his hand. Mana gathered at his fingertips, shimmering violet-blue. He shaped the energy, let it build in his chest, and snapped it forward.

The *Arcane Blast* burst from his fingertip and struck the dummy with a satisfying crack, dispersing in a flash of force and sparks. Not bad. Cleaner than before. He was beginning to feel it—but he hadn't found his rhythm just yet, the flow that would make it second nature.

He stepped back, adjusted his stance, and let the mana flow through him. He opened his eyes and unleashed an *Arcane Explosion*—a shockwave of glowing force that surged from his core and expanded outward with startling speed, rippling through the air, shredding a few floating leaves and sending a pair of startled birds tumbling from a nearby tree.

A fine layer of arcane residue drifted through the air as the blast faded.

Emric glanced at the not-hurt-but-clearly-annoyed birds and muttered, "Sorry," knowing full well they couldn't understand him.

He exhaled. *I'm getting there*, he thought.

"You know, I thought I was the only one who came up here."

Emric flinched slightly and looked around, startled.

Madi stood at the edge of the platform, holding a mostly empty takeout container and a bottle of lemonade. Her crimson hair was windblown, and she wore a dark gray hoodie—casual, relaxed, like this wasn't the first time she'd wandered off alone.

"I didn't mean to sneak up on you," she said quickly, raising a hand. "You looked like you were in the zone."

Emric chuckled. "It's all good. I get carried away when I'm focusing. I found this place and figured no one really came around here."

“That’s why I like it here,” she said, stepping closer and glancing around. “No crowds, no noise. Sometimes Mrs. Atkinson walks her little Yorkie by—but that’s about it.”

Emric smiled faintly. “That’s what I was hoping for. No noise. Everything’s just... so loud lately. I need time to breathe. Time to just listen.”

“I come here when I need to think,” Madi said, brushing a bit of hair behind her ear. “My house is... a lot sometimes. Big personalities. This place gives me breathing room.”

Emric glanced down at his hands. “Same. It’s the only place I don’t feel like I’m being watched all the time.”

Madi tilted her head. “You don’t talk much at school.”

“Neither do you,” he replied.

She grinned. “Usually only when the professors call on me. I like to stay out of the way. I’m not one for the spotlight.”

“I hear that,” Emric said.

“Sometimes I think the loudest people are just trying to convince themselves they belong,” she said. “But the quiet ones—” she looked at him, eyes steady, “—we’re just trying to survive without going insane.”

She gave a quiet laugh at her own words.

Emric’s brow lifted a bit. He hadn’t expected that.

“Yeah,” he said. “That’s exactly it.”

Madi sat down on the edge of the platform, legs swinging. "Mind if I stay a while?"

Emric shrugged. "Not at all."

She set her container aside and leaned back on her hands, watching the clouds drift lazily above the city.

"You've got good casting form, by the way. I could tell earlier—in Moss's class, when you cast the mana missile. It was pretty clear you've done that before."

Emric rubbed the back of his neck. "Thanks. I've watched my older brother practice for years, and I just copy what he does."

It wasn't true—but he didn't want to talk about the quiet afternoons he'd spent practicing beside his mother.

"Well..." she said with a small smirk, "you look like someone who was trying to get it perfect before showing it off."

Emric scratched the back of his ear. "I'm not really the 'show-off' type," he said.

"I guessed that much," she replied. "That's what makes it interesting."

They sat together for a while—quiet, comfortable. Neither of them felt the need to fill the silence.

Until Madi finally asked, "So... why did you wait so long to pick a Crest?"

Emric hesitated for a second.

The question was so casual, so innocent—but his chest tightened immediately.

He was supposed to pick it with his mom. She'd promised him.

And every time he thought about it afterward, all he felt was the space she left behind.

He opened his mouth. Nothing came out.

Panic flared in his chest.

He glanced around, searching for something—anything—to change the subject.

"I—uh—Tamlin invited me to be on his team for the school tournament," he blurted out.

His brain immediately screamed: *OH CRAP. I'M NOT SUPPOSED TO KNOW ABOUT THAT YET.*

Madi blinked. "What tournament?"

Emric froze.

"I—uh—he said I wasn't supposed to say anything yet. I think it's being announced at the assembly tomorrow. He talked about how they're going to have teams, and he wanted me."

Madi stared at him, mouth slightly open.

Then, to his surprise, she grinned.

"Ohhh. So what you're actually telling me is that I cannot trust you with any of my secrets."

She laughed.

Emric groaned softly and buried his face in his hands. "Ugh. Please pretend like I didn't say anything. I can't believe I just—ugh."

"Nope. Too late. You said it. It's out there now." She continued cheerfully, "Besides... it's kind of cute when you panic."

He peeked through his fingers. "I wasn't panicking."

"You absolutely were."

Emric sighed, defeated. She was right. He was totally panicking.

And despite himself, Emric smiled.

He dropped his hands and cleared his throat, searching for another way to change the subject. "What about you? What Crest did you pick?"

Madi blinked, caught off guard by the sudden shift—but she didn't seem to mind.

"I chose the Crest of Mind," she said, smiling.

He nodded. "How come you chose that one?"

She leaned back on her hands again, looking thoughtful. “I’ve always had a good memory. Not photographic or anything, but when I learn something, it sticks.”

She paused, glancing down at her hoodie.

“That’s part of the reason I was drawn to it over the others. But it’s not the main reason I picked it.”

Emric tilted his head, curious.

“I love sewing,” Madi said simply. “Making things. I’ve always liked taking something plain and turning it into something useful—or beautiful. Or both.”

Her fingers toyed with the hem of her sleeve.

“Enchanting was the next step. Once I figured out I could take regular stuff and give it magical properties... I was totally hooked.”

She smiled, eyes lighting up.

“The best part? I get to blend other domains into what I make. I’ve used flame runes for warmth, essence threads for healing—even a little surge magic to reinforce stitching. There’s nothing else like it.”

She tugged at the edge of her hoodie.

“This? It’s enchanted. Doesn’t matter if it’s a blizzard or a heat wave—this hoodie makes it feel like it’s always seventy degrees.”

Emric’s eyebrows rose. “Seriously?”

“Seriously,” she said with a grin. “Perfect temperature, all the time. Best thing I’ve ever made.”

He gave a quiet, appreciative nod. “That’s... incredibly cool.”

Madi shrugged like it was no big deal, but her smile lingered.

“Thanks,” she said. “Not everyone thinks enchanting is that exciting, but I don’t care. I love it. It’s like... crafting little pieces of order in a chaotic world.”

They fell into silence again, both enjoying the peace.

The hum of the dampening field, the breeze slipping past the edge of the terrace—it all faded into the background. For a moment, Emric didn’t feel the weight of needing to prove anything.

He was just... there.

Eventually, he realized it was getting late and let out a quiet sigh.

“I should probably go,” he said, rising to his feet. “It’s my turn to make dinner tonight.”

Madi stood as well, brushing her hands off on her skirt.

“Yeah, I should head back. My folks are probably wondering where I went off to.”

She smiled as she turned to leave. “See ya tomorrow... when the school announces something nobody knows anything about.”

Emric groaned. “You’re not letting that go, are you?”

“Nope,” she said, not turning around—but he could hear the smile in her voice.

He just shook his head, still smiling. They walked away, heading in separate directions.

Emric’s thoughts drifted back to something she’d said earlier:

Besides... it’s kind of cute when you panic.

He blinked.

Then his face flushed bright red.

Did she just call me cute?

Chapter 8

A loud screech of magical feedback jolted half the auditorium. Students winced, and a few covered their ears.

The enchanted banners overhead flickered in the rafters near the ceiling.

Emric relaxed in his seat, his ears finally done ringing from the feedback.

He refocused his attention toward the front of the auditorium, where Mrs. Atkinson stood behind the podium. Now that he wasn't quite as nervous as he'd been on his first day, he realized just how old she was.

She wasn't seventy or seventy-five. She was old-old. Like, *"I love you, Gam Gam, but how are you still alive?"* old.

She looked like someone's eccentric grandmother had wandered into a staff meeting and no one had the heart to ask her to leave.

"Hello, students of Cloudrest!" came the slow, deliberate voice of Mrs. Atkinson, the school's long-serving receptionist. "And hello to any faculty members still pretending not to nap in the back row—I see you, Professor Kettlebrand."

A light ripple of chuckles passed through the room.

Emric glanced to his left. Tamlin was grinning from ear to ear. He clearly knew what the assembly was about—and thanks to Tamlin's excitement, so did Emric. And because of Emric... Madi knew too.

"Now," Mrs. Atkinson continued, "before I bring out our new principal, I just wanted to update you all and tell you Mr. Pickles is doing much better. He is, however, still wearing his cone of shame."

She paused, frowning slightly, as if she'd just walked into a room and forgotten why. Then she perked up, nodding to herself.

"I remember when I was a girl, they never made dogs wear those cones of shame. Once, we were on vacation in California—we were there to see killer whales at SeaWorld. But when we got there, I needed a new heel for my shoe, so I took a walk to find a shoe repair shop. We called those 'cobblers' back then, you know."

Tamlin leaned forward and whispered, "Here we go."

"So, I tied a carrot to my fluxbag—which was the style at the time—and set off down the road. But the road had a toll, five orbs, and in those days, orbs were green, and we'd say, 'Give me a hundred greenies for a sigil,' which we thought was very clever."

Emric blinked slowly.

"Now, where were we? Oh, yes—the important thing was that I had a carrot on my fluxbag, which was the style at the time. They only had orange carrots because of the drought. You couldn't get an onion."

Emric turned to Tamlin.

Tamlin just nodded. "She does this a lot."

Offstage to her left, someone cleared their throat—firmly, and with rising urgency.

"Oh! That's right," Mrs. Atkinson chirped. "Today marks the official announcement of your new principal... Principal Albrecht Grimm."

She motioned grandly to the right.

Principal Grimm appeared stage left.

It took her a moment to notice.

Then, with a delighted laugh, she turned around and gave him an awkward hug—one he neither returned nor resisted.

She began to walk away from the podium... in the wrong direction.

Grimm, without a word, gently took her elbow and steered her toward the side exit, preventing her from marching straight off the front of the stage.

He stepped up to the podium, adjusted it slightly, and cleared his throat.

"Thank you, Mrs. Atkinson," he said flatly. "That was... comprehensive."

He looked out over the sea of students—calm, poised, and unreadable. His hair was short and clean-cut, with clear strands of gray running through it. His clothing was perfectly pressed. He didn't move when he talked, like a statue that had been programmed to deliver announcements.

"I'm Principal Albrecht Grimm. Two items are on the agenda for today: expectations and opportunities."

He paused. Not for effect—just long enough to make it uncomfortable.

"Expectations," he said. "Your mana tags are to be kept visible on your person at all times. No hostile casting outside sanctioned spaces. Mind magic requires affirmative consent. Transfiguration above tier two is restricted to lab zones. If you injure someone, the wards will be able to heal them. Unfortunately, the wards cannot heal your GPA."

A few students laughed nervously. Grimm did not.

"Opportunities," he continued. "This semester, we're launching the *Cloudrest Trials*—a cross-discipline tournament designed to measure teamwork, control, and real-world application of magic."

He raised his hand. Lines of pale blue light stitched themselves into the air above the stage—three clean, minimal runes hovered in an arc.

"Team Objective Lane Battler."

A bracket appeared in the first rune as he gestured, with the letters *PvP* above the bracket.

"The Aether Gauntlet."

He gestured to the next rune, and an outline of a maze spiraling downward in a cone formed, with the letters *PvE* above it.

"And finally," he said, still utterly flat, "a Colossus hunt."

He gestured at the third and final rune as it shifted into the silhouette of a giant creature, with the letters *PvPvE* glowing above it.

Murmurs rippled through the hall. Tamlin practically vibrated in his chair.

"Teams of five," Grimm said, "one optional alternate. Rosters lock in one week from today. Safety wards will be active. Stupidity wards are not a thing, so they will not be active."

A ripple of laughter broke out. Grimm didn't blink.

"All events are weighted. You can't brute-force your way through them. Smart strategy and team composition will give you an advantage."

"The winning team receives a Spire Commendation, interviews for apprenticeship placements, and fifty Sigils. Also—bragging rights. I'm told those are very important."

He continued with no inflection at all. Emric wasn't sure if he was joking or not; he was finding this principal very hard to read.

"Registration opens tomorrow. See Mrs. Atkinson for sign-ups."

Grimm stepped back from the podium. "That is all. Make good choices. Get to class." He exited stage left.

The student body sat there for a beat, confused and unsure if that was really the end of the assembly. It seemed short—but that was it. One by one, they began filing out toward their classrooms.

Back in Professor Beck's class, he clapped his hands once. The chatter stopped.

"All right," he said, leaning against the desk. "Let's hear it. Questions?"

For once, Tamlin didn't fire first.

Emric's hand went up.

Beck nodded. "Mister Vale."

"What exactly did Principal Grimm mean by a Team Objective Lane Battler?"

Beck blinked, faintly amused. "Fair question." He glanced at the ceiling for a moment. "Fastest way to explain it... anyone played *League of Legends*, *Dota*, or *Heroes of the Storm*?"

Most of the class made sounds of recognition. Someone in the back muttered, "I'm bronze by choice," which earned a few laughs.

"For those who haven't," Beck said, sketching a sigil in the air. Illusory light bloomed over the amphitheater—a floating map appeared, three long paths linking two glowing anchors, with a shimmering river of mana cutting through the center. Small lantern-like towers winked into being along each lane.

"Five versus five," Beck explained. "Two sides. Call them Azure and Crimson." The bases pulsed on opposite corners. "Each side has a Keystone—think of it as a core, the big glowing 'do not break' thing. There are three lanes—top, mid, bottom—" the paths blinked in turn "—and the wilds between them. *League* players call it the jungle."

"In the wilds," he continued, "faculty-conjured elementals and neutral objectives wait to be captured. Clear them for temporary boosts to your magic, vision, or pressure on the map."

"At the start, you'll fan out to lanes. Shortly after, waves of arcane automata—your minions—march down all three lanes from both sides." Knee-high golems assembled and trundled forward. "They do one trick: walk and punch whatever's red."

He tapped the lane lanterns. "Ward pylons, or towers. These will shoot at you if you're on the wrong side. They're your team's defenses, and they double as territory markers.

Destroy theirs to push the battle line forward. Lose yours, and you'll get shoved back."

A few heads nodded as it began to click.

"You'll fight enemy players and their constructs," Beck went on. "Win skirmishes, secure objectives, earn enhancements that make your spells and team stronger. The goal isn't to win the coolest duel in mid. The goal is to open a path, collapse their defenses, and destroy the enemy Keystone." The far core dimmed and shattered into light. "Do that, you win the round."

He let the map spin once, then dismissed it with a flick of his hand. "That's the shape of it. Lanes, wilds, waves, pylons, Keystone. Objectives over ego. Questions?"

The girl with orange glasses and a dark braid over one shoulder raised her hand—the same one Emric had noticed on his first day.

"Are there... like roles? Or do we just run around and hope we win?"

"Please don't 'just run around and hope,'" Beck said, smiling faintly. "A common composition helps. People call them different things, but the idea is the same. You'll need a tank to anchor fights, damage dealers, utility mages, and healers. You're not required to copy that composition—but ignore balance at your own peril."

Murmurs spread. Tamlin was getting visibly more and more excited.

Madi raised her hand, hesitant. "What about personal enchantments?"

"Those will be allowed," Beck said. "If one team has a mage with the Crest of Mind who specializes in enchantments, that team may have an advantage over one that doesn't. That said, there are many ways to gain the upper hand."

Tamlin couldn't contain his excitement. He blurted out a one-word question: "Potions?"

"Consumables are allowed," Beck confirmed. "Which also ties back to strategy. If you have an alchemist on your team, that's an edge over one that doesn't. Like I said—ignore balance at your own peril."

Emric was already thinking strategy. "The team size is five, with one alternate. Can we alternate mid-game?"

"Alternates may sub on a safe timer," Beck said. "When a teammate is downed and waiting to respawn at the fountain, your captain can call a swap. But note the risk—if you planned for Mage A to replace Mage B, and Mage C goes down first, Mage A replaces Mage C. Plan accordingly."

A boy with spiky hair stood up. "Are faculty... playing?"

"No," Beck said. "We will, however, be the ones piloting certain neutral elements on the map."

The school bell chimed. Chairs scraped. Backpacks zipped closed.

Tamlin leaned across the aisle toward Emric the instant they were dismissed. “Okay,” he said, brimming with his usual enthusiasm. “We need to get at least three more people—but preferably four.”

As the students funneled into the hallway, the excitement was almost visible in the air.

Emric thought about what Beck had said—that teams with an enchanter would have an advantage over teams without one. And he knew exactly where to find a mage who could give them that edge.

He looked at Tamlin. “I have an idea for someone who should be on our team, and I need to ask her before it’s too late.” Then he took off down the hall in search of Madi.

Tamlin blinked, then grinned. “That’s the spirit,” he said to himself. “I’ll go find someone who enjoys getting punched.” He finger-gunned toward the door and disappeared into the hallway chaos.

Emric squeezed through the commotion, scanning for a flash of crimson hair. He spotted her slipping out the side door, dashed through a gap, and caught up.

“Hey,” he said, slightly out of breath.

She looked up, her green eyes bright in the sunlight. “Hey. I guess your inside information was correct. I wasn’t expecting *that* much, though—it’s kind of exciting.”

"Yeah," Emric said. "Listen, have you thought about your team yet?"

"Do you want to be on my team?" she asked eagerly.

"You're already on a team?" Emric asked, caught off guard.

"Yeah. Me and my best friend, Kennedy," Madi replied happily. "She's got the Crest of Bloom and she's an amazing mender. If we had you, we'd only need a couple more."

"I have an idea," Emric said quickly. "Tamlin and I are forming up as well. We should join the two teams together to make four. Then we'd only need one or two more."

"Okay, that sounds good," Madi said with a smile—a beautiful smile, Emric realized. He hadn't noticed before how much he liked it.

"Awesome." Emric felt his cheeks warm. "I'll tell Tamlin the good news."

He turned to leave, but Madi held up her mana tag. "Wait. Let's tap tags so we can talk outside of class."

Emric blushed even harder. He was about to exchange tag info with a girl—holy crap.

He tried to look smooth, pulling his tag from his pocket, but the corner caught. He fumbled it, juggling the tag between his hands for a solid two seconds before finally catching it.

Madi giggled and held her tag closer.

Emric noticed a faint blush in her cheeks as he tapped his tag to hers.

Their tags chimed once—*link confirmed.*

Chapter 9

Emric entered the apartment, still grinning from actually getting mana tag info from a girl. He still couldn't believe it.

The living room was dim except for the pale glow of the aetherplate. Kael lay half-sunk into the sofa, boots off, coat thrown over the armrest, a takeout carton teetering on the edge of the side table. His attention was locked on the news.

"—and authorities confirm there were no injuries," the anchor said. "Credit goes to Hunter Cromwell, the number four–ranked mage in America—better known as the Maestro—whose harmonic casting de-escalated a riot at a soccer stadium in under three minutes."

The image shifted to a wide shot of the stadium dissolving into chaos—shouts, shoves, a firebolt streaking red across the air—then a single tone rolled through the stands, low and pure. Lines of light braided above the pitch, weaving into a symphony of magic. The crowd stilled; people blinked, shoulders lowering, their anger softening into quiet humming as if they all remembered the same lullaby at once.

The anchor continued, "Cromwell, a Crest of Mind specialist in resonance magic, layered a *Concord Hymn* through the venue, calming the crowd while mages from the Pillar of Authority cleared the exits. Menders from the Pillar of Preservation were standing by but, thankfully, weren't needed."

Control like that made Emric's freshly practiced Arcane Blast feel like a sparkler.

"Hey," Emric called.

Kael didn't look away. He lifted one hand from the cushion—half a wave, half a twitch—and set it back down.

Emric stood there a moment, the grin slowly fading. He dropped his bag by the door and moved closer, stopping at the edge of the sofa. On-screen, Cromwell—hair tied back—spoke briefly to reporters without a trace of arrogance. The caption beneath him read: *MAESTRO: "MUSIC IS A BRIDGE."*

Kael finally exhaled. "Music has a way of calming the masses," he said, sounding worn thin from work. "No panic. No casualties. Thirty thousand people, and he threads the needle."

"Yeah," Emric said quietly, feeling it in his chest.

Silence stretched while the aetherplate droned softly in the background.

"So—uh—Cloudrest announced a tournament today," Emric said, trying for casual. "Teams of five, match-based. They're calling it a Team Objective Lane Battler. I was asked to join a team."

That caught Kael's attention. His gaze slid toward Emric. "Who asked you?"

"The class peer leader—Tamlin. I think you'd like him. He also chose the Crest of Iron, but unlike you, he specializes in alchemy and focuses on strange potions."

Kael stared. "Fantastic," he said dryly. "A walking hazard cart." He rubbed his brow like he was shooing away a headache. "So he asked you? Not 'We'll call you if someone sprains an ankle.' Actually asked you?"

Emric felt heat crawl up his neck. "Actually asked me," he said.

Kael leaned back on the couch, annoyed more than anything else, eyes drifting toward the aetherplate. "Well… congratulations on being…" He searched for the word. "Recruitable." He waved it off. "Do whatever you want. I don't care if you play your student war games."

Emric muttered under his breath, hoping Kael wouldn't hear. "You sound thrilled."

"I sound tired," Kael replied flatly. "And if people are depending on you, you'd better not let them down this time." The last two words dripping with venom.

"I won't. I'm working on it," Emric said, jaw tight.

"Work faster." Kael's tone hardened, then evened out again. "If you're really on a team, don't make them babysit you."

Emric blinked. "You just said you didn't care."

"I don't," Kael said, annoyed because he clearly did a little. "But if my brother's going to be on the field, he's carrying the name of Vale with him. So he'd better live up to that name."

Emric looked down slightly. "I will," he said.

"Good," Kael replied.

Emric picked up his bag and walked into the kitchen, where Nia was rifling through the cupboards in a mild panic.

"What's wrong?" he asked.

"We're out of moondrops, and the only things left are fruit and—" She turned to him, horrified. "Vegetables."

"You can't just eat candy!" Kael's annoyed voice came from the other room.

Nia scrunched her face in Kael's general direction—he couldn't see it anyway—then sighed in defeat and dropped into a chair, thunking her forehead against the table.

Emric flinched. "Didn't that hurt?"

"Nothing else matters until I get my candy," she said dramatically.

"So… how about that school assembly?" Emric offered, hoping to steer her mind away from sugar.

"Right?!" She popped her head up. "Mrs. Atkinson is a gem, and I cannot get a read on the new principal. Was he mad the whole time? And who came up with the tournament idea? That didn't sound like him at all. It sounded like you up there—talking about how the tournament focuses on head-to-head matches and cooperative challenges. That's gamer talk, not educator talk."

"When Tamlin asked you to be on his team the other day, I had no idea it was going to be *that* big of a deal," she added.

"Me either," Emric said. "But I'm going to do my best. We've got four people so far, so we just need one more."

"Oh really?" Nia perked up. "I thought it was just you and Tamlin. Did you actually make new friends?"

Emric blushed and rubbed the back of his neck. "Yeah, I… sort of asked this girl, Madi, to join our team. She's an enchanter, so I figured we could get an edge with enchanted gear. And her friend's a mender, which rounds us out pretty well."

But Nia wasn't listening to any of that. She narrowed her eyes, a smirk creeping up her face. "Why are you blushing?" she asked, all sing-song and knowing.

"Gah." Emric scrambled for an excuse. "No reason. It's just… hot in the kitchen. Someone must be using the oven."

"The oven's off," Nia said, smirk unshaken.

"Well, I should, uh, go," Emric muttered, pushing up from his chair and angling for the hallway.

He made it one step before Nia caught his arm and shoved him back into the chair with surprising force for her small frame.

"Spill," she said, eyes bright with excitement. "Who's Madi?"

Emric stared at the table grain for a long second, mind racing for an escape—but he knew he was trapped. "There's this girl who's… really nice and funny," he admitted finally. "We talked a bit over the weekend. She found me on the floating practice terrace at the park while I was working on some of the new spells from the tomes we bought."

"Mhm. And what were you practicing when Miss Nice-and-Funny wandered over?"

"Arcane Blast and Arcane Explosion." He could hear how eager he sounded and tried to tone it down. "I was keeping my form tight—concentrating the arcane into a single point at my fingertip so it hit as clean as possible."

"What did you talk about?" Nia pressed, hungry for details.

"We both like that quiet part of the park. It helps drown out the city noise," he said with a shrug. "She also said she was surprised it took me so long to pick a Crest—especially after how well I cast the scroll in Moss's class."

From the living room, Kael called, "She wasn't the only one."

"Shut up," Nia shot back, then leaned in, elbows on the table. "So, you two just talked?"

"We talked about school," Emric said. "I, uh, accidentally told her about the tournament before it was announced. And today we… tapped tags." He instantly regretted adding that last part.

Nia squealed. "Mana tag exchange?"

"That's a normal thing to do," Emric said, trying not to sound like it was one of the biggest achievements of his life.

Nia slapped the table, delighted. "She sounds perfect for you! Kind, funny, loves quiet places—just like you. Brother, these are all green flags."

"It's not— I mean, it's just— we're building a team!"

"Uh-huh," Nia said, practically vibrating out of her chair. "I *cannot wait* to tell Katie!" she added before darting out of the kitchen and into her room.

Emric sat there for a moment, blank. Then he picked up his backpack and headed to his room.

Kael's words wouldn't let go: if he was carrying the Vale name, he'd better live up to it.

His mother had been terrifyingly strong. His father—until recently—was one of the most respected menders in the Pillar of Preservation. And now Kael was carving out a name in the Pillar of Industry. Vale carried weight. Kael was right: he couldn't be the embarrassment.

Another line surfaced in his head: *Don't make them babysit you.*

Later that night, he finally set his bag on the bed. The apartment had fallen into that late-night hush. He rolled his shoulder to work the soreness free, cleared a space on his desk, and tapped the aetherplate on the wall. The crystal core flickered awake with a soft blue glow, and a floating interface shimmered to life across the room.

No new message from Miles this time.

Emric opened the Aethergrid and started searching for how to use Arcane magic in a team setting—calm coordination, clean timing, protective casting when someone else overextends. That sort of thing.

He found a few solid guides and began to read. *Breathe before you shape. Keep your hands loose. Announce what you're doing. Let your power gather lower in the chest, not in the shoulders.* Practical stuff.

On one page, a diagram showed a basic force weave—three strokes, then release. Emric traced the pattern in the air without casting, just teaching his muscles the path. The aetherplate hummed softly in the background. His mana tag glowed faintly blue on the edge of his bag.

He moved his hands through a focusing pattern meant to steady his mind and feel the mana's flow through the web—without actually conjuring. The familiar tingle rose, clean and contained, letting him trace the current without forming a spell.

Anchor first.

What? he thought, pausing. He didn't know where that thought had come from.

Whatever, he thought, and reset his hands to try again. He breathed slower, steadier.

Anchor first.

There it was again. His brow furrowed. *What is going on?*

This time, he shifted his stance—feet wider, weight lower, shoulders loose—anchored to the floor.

He traced the same pattern. The current surged, clearer than before. For a heartbeat, he could actually *see* it—fine threads of light gathering at his center, flowing down his arms, pooling at his fingertips. Not just a feeling, but a map of the flow itself.

It was incredible. What was *going on?* His mind raced.

Two beats.

He held the shape, then released.

A coin's worth of force drifted into the air—no flash, no scorch—just a soft pressure that lifted the corner of a page and set it down again. Neat and tidy.

He tried again, smaller this time. *In—two. Hold—two. Out—four. Anchor first.*

A pea-sized pulse kissed the desk and vanished like a breath.

He set a crumpled receipt on the rim of his wastebasket, centered his stance, whispered, “Steady,” and nudged. The paper tipped and dropped cleanly inside.

Emric let himself grin.

He didn’t need to name whatever had clicked. He could feel it in his hands, in the looseness of his shoulders, in the way the energy settled where it belonged.

The aetherplate dimmed to a faint halo as he shut it off. He lay back, breathing in that same steady rhythm he’d found at the desk.

Anchor first, he thought—not a rule so much as a habit taking root.

The room went still.

He fell asleep smiling.

Chapter 10

The Bloom Wing of Cloudrest's teaching garden hummed like a sleeping beehive. Herb beds stepped up in green terraces, leaves beaded with ward-dew; pale Ward Lanterns hung from iron crooks, pulsing with the dampening field and quietly sniffing the air for pollen and toxins. Beyond the stretch of greenhouses, a Toxin Hood exhaled a faint alkaloid tang. A bank of carnivorous plants blinked their patient mouths open and shut. The sun angled low across the beds, turning the soil bronze and lighting the lanterns like small moons.

Madi led the way down the gravel path, hoodie sleeves pushed to her elbows. "She's usually out here after school," she said, with Emric close behind, easing a quiet ache in his shoulder from last night's drills.

They rounded a hedge turn and found her: a tall girl with dark hair in a single braid over one shoulder, eyes shut behind orange-framed glasses catching the light. Between her hands hovered a Verdance Kernel—a perfect green sphere, clear as bottled spring, humming faintly like a glass rim. The air was thick enough with magic that her braid lifted from her shoulder and hung just above it.

Madi lifted a finger to her lips. Emric nodded and took one last step—onto a dry stick.

In the garden's hush, the snap sounded like the world's biggest sheet of bubble wrap going off at once.

Emric flinched. Madi's eyes went wide and a grin tried to escape her face. Kennedy's eyes opened, the calm of her meditation clipped by annoyance. "Oh. It's you," she said—still annoyed, but in the register that said she'd actually have to meet a new person, even if they shared homeroom.

Madi's voice was warm. "I brought him."

Kennedy's gaze hopped from Madi to Emric and pinned him. She slid her orange frames up her nose with the tip of a finger. "Emric Vale." Not a question. He'd noticed her a few times in class; no wonder she'd asked whether the tournament would have defined roles. If she was Bloom, she'd be thinking about team balance.

"Madi says you want to join forces—merge your team with ours," Kennedy said, still not standing. "I don't agree to anything without seeing people in person."

After another long look up and down, she rose. The annoyance didn't leave her face; maybe she just had RAF—resting annoyed face.

She stepped in, and Madi eased back to give her space. Kennedy circled Emric once. Twice. On the third pass, she stopped a step away, measuring.

"I saw your spellwork in Moss's lab when you blew that training dummy apart," she said. "That doesn't mean I approve of you. I only team with people who can use their brains, not just magic."

Emric swallowed. "How can I prove how smart I am?" He blinked. "Are you gonna give me a math problem?"

Kennedy raised a finger, in an important-point pose—when a shout cut across the beds from the gate where he and Madi had come in.

"Crew!" Tamlin's voice spilled over the herbs, thrilled and breathless. "Found you—and look who I brought!" He barreled in, half-dragging another student by the collar of his shirt.

The student he hauled was taller than Emric by a head, but much, much slimmer—maybe ninety pounds, soaking wet.

Tamlin let go and presented him like a model on *The Price Is Right.* "Pax Greaves," he announced, beaming.

Pax didn't quite meet anyone's eyes. "Hello."

Kennedy tilted her head. "Hi, Pax." She and Madi exchanged a quick, puzzled look.

Emric stepped forward. "Hey, Pax, how's it going? Gotta be honest—you don't look like you've been in many fights, let alone led a team into a match."

Pax didn't say anything.

Tamlin bounced in without a hint of nerves. "Oh, he's capable of being the tip of the spear, for sure. He's the walking definition of 'don't judge a book by its cover.' He's just got some stage fright."

Emric sized him up again, a smirk tugging at his mouth. "What's your Crest?"

Pax lifted his pendant. "The Crest of Elements."

Emric nodded. He looked past the metal to Pax's eyes. "You don't talk much, do you?"

Pax shook his head.

"Well, if Tamlin trusts you, so do I," Emric said. "What element do you specialize in?"

Without a word, Pax bent, spreading his palms to the soil.

The earth boiled up his arms like a swarm of tiny creatures. In a heartbeat, he looked like a mud man, and then he rose, the shape growing with him. Stone layered on, coarse and uneven, and he swelled until he stood nearly thirteen feet tall—lopsided, the left side of his body much thicker than the right.

As he stood, Tamlin had an *I told you so* kind of grin on his face.

Emric craned his neck. "Are you left-handed?"

Pax grunted an affirmative.

"I can tell," Emric said. "You have a hard time regulating mana through your body; you're over-channeling through your dominant hand. That's why you're lopsided."

Kennedy's eyebrows lifted. Madi's did, too.

"My mother was an Elementalist as well—fire specialty—but the principles carry over," Emric said, feeling the heat in his cheeks at their looks. "I thought I'd be just like her, so I studied that domain for years." He scratched the back of his head.

He moved to Pax's side, voice easing into instruction. "Elements aren't about domination; you're a conduit. Send mana down and ask the earth to meet you. Respect and communication, not muscle."

Pax, the mud man, stared at him with a look of confusion.

He glanced up. "We'll do it together. Can you drop your spell?"

Pax nodded, and the mud sank away. He shrank back to his normal size.

Emric went up and stood shoulder to shoulder with Pax. "Anchor first," Emric said, setting a neutral stance. Pax mirrored him.

Emric closed his eyes. New York. Training with his mother on a rooftop garden warmed by late-afternoon sun. Her hands shaping his. *Ask, don't force.* He hadn't touched elemental work since she died. Casting a firebolt from a scroll in Moss's lab wasn't the same as this—real casting. He'd forgotten how much he missed it.

He knelt and pressed his palm to the bed's edge. "Don't force the earth to encompass you; send your mana into the ground and ask it to aid you." Both boys pulsed mana into the ground.

The Ward Lanterns brightened, and the dampening field gave a warning thrum.

Kennedy winced. "Careful—the Bloom dampener reports mana spikes. If it chirps twice, the steward shows up."

Stone climbed Pax evenly this time, plating over his arms, chest, then crown. A balanced golem stood where the lopsided one had wobbled a minute before—thirteen feet of steady, deliberate mass.

Madi exhaled and laughed. Tamlin fist-pumped. Kennedy let out a slow breath. "Alright, you've convinced me—but don't make me regret it." Her eyes never left Pax.

The Ward Lanterns continued to brighten until an alarm sounded through the garden, and a Speaking Rune crackled to life: "What in the world is going on here? We recorded an overload in the garden!"

A crackle of electricity, then a zap, and a boy—clearly still a student—appeared. He wore a slate workshop coat and had a clipboard. He had a strange device around his wrist. The clipboard wasn't a normal clipboard, though; it had magical runes flowing like a seismograph during an 8.5.

"Who authorized a thirteen-foot earth form in the teaching garden?" he said, sounding like the most stressed-out person in the history of the world.

Emric looked at Tamlin, then at the newcomer. "Nobody?"

He tapped the device on his wrist, and the lanterns settled back to a polite glow. "Do you know how much paperwork I'm going to have to fill out for this report?"

Tamlin stepped forward. "My name is Tamlin, the peer leader for Professor Beck's homeroom. Who are you?"

The student looked panicked for a second, then regained his composure and said, with far too much bravado, "My name isn't important—but you know what *is* important? Following rules!" He hit his clipboard as he said the final word.

"I am the student ward for this wing," he said. "And Fabrication Lab Liaison. But that's not important."

Madi's face registered recognition. "Wait, I know you," she said.

The student's eyes went wide; he tried to regain composure. "That's impossible," he said, trying to hide the fear in his voice.

"Yes, you're the guy who projected etiquette scores over everyone's head in the lunchroom," Madi said.

Kennedy looked appalled. "That was you? I do *not* slurp my soup!"

“Behavioral feedback improves civility!” the student shot back.

“Wait,” Emric said. “What happened?”

Even Tamlin looked at the student, annoyed.

The boy swallowed. “It was a pilot. A very short pilot. The ‘Manners Meter’ assigned labels to nudge improvements—‘Slurper,’ ‘Fork Drummer,’ ‘Elbow Tyrant,’ ‘Napkin Hero’—purely informational.”

“It crowned me ‘Sip Slurper Supreme,’” Kennedy said flatly.

“And it dinged me every time I tapped my fork,” Tamlin added.

Madi narrowed her eyes. “And it called me a ‘Napkin Goblin.’ Which is… not a thing.”

The Ward Lanterns, still a shade too bright, pulsed. He tapped the device on his wrist; the glow settled to a polite moonlight.

“I’m sorry,” he said. “It was an experiment that got out of hand, and I’m sorry.”

“You did that to every student in the school?” Emric asked.

The student nodded.

Emric’s eyes narrowed. “What’s your name?”

“Zebulon Quibble,” Zebulon responded.

Everyone stared at him, startled by the name.

"I hate it," he said. "I told you it wasn't important."

"Well, what do your friends call you?" Emric asked.

"After what happened in the lunchroom, I don't really have friends anymore," Zebulon responded.

Emric let out an exasperated huff. "Yeah, I can believe that," he said, grinning. "That was a big deal. How did you do that to every single student in the school?"

"Technically," Zebulon said, "it wasn't just students; it hit faculty too."

A smile crossed Emric's face. "How did you pull that off? Didn't the teachers know how to stop it?"

A grin spread across Zebulon's face. "For me, it was pretty easy. I specialize in making gadgets that tell me information. I attached a small detector charm under each table that measured diners' habits and projected labels to help them understand and improve their table manners. I also cloaked the detector charms so they had to be found with a specific ward spell that isn't common knowledge. I make things like that all the time."

Everyone looked at him, impressed.

Emric's mind clicked. "Do you have a team for the tournament?"

Zebulon looked horrified. "I do not want anything to do with that tournament. I'd get absolutely wrecked out there."

“What? Why?” Emric asked.

“Everybody hates me after that, and I’m sure the only reason people would want me on the field is so they could blow me up,” Zebulon said sadly.

“I can understand that,” Emric said. “Too bad. I think any team with your inventions would have a big advantage. I was going to ask you to join our team.”

Madi, Kennedy, Pax, and Tamlin all looked at Emric, scandalized.

“Why?” Zebulon asked. “So you can set me up and let the other team smash me into the ground? No thank you!”

“No, I’m thinking if we had access to some of your inventions, we’d have a big advantage,” Emric replied.

“Well, too bad,” Zebulon said. “You’ll never get me out on that field.” He looked down, then added quietly, “But I will envy the winners of the tournament. I really wanted an apprenticeship interview with the Pillar of Industry—that’s my dream.”

Emric’s eyes narrowed, and his mouth curled into a smile. “What about this: you’re on our team, but you don’t compete. You supply us with some of your inventions, and if we win, you get that apprenticeship opportunity?”

Zebulon’s eyes narrowed, considering the offer. “You want me on your team? And I wouldn’t have to be in danger?”

“You just have to be at the event,” Emric said. “You don’t actually have to be on the field to be part of the team, and your contribution would be the gear.”

Kennedy folded her arms. “Wait, don’t we have a say in this?”

“Yeah, of course,” Emric said quickly. “I was just thinking out loud and got lost in my thoughts.”

Tamlin grinned. “Well, I think it’s a great idea. Think about all the cool things Zebulon could make for us.”

Madi said, “Zebulon is too long to say all the time, so I’m just gonna call you Zeb.”

Kennedy looked at the rest of the team, and even Pax looked approving. “Fine,” she said. “But no more Manners Meter experiments—or anything like that.”

“You don’t have to worry about that,” Zeb said, hands raised in surrender.

“Are you sure you want me on your team?” Zeb asked Emric.

Emric held out his hand.

Zeb stared at the hand like it was a contract, then shook it.

Emric smiled. “Welcome to the team, Zeb.”

Chapter 11

The magic ink was already drying, curling into spidery sigils across the scroll Emric held. All they needed was a name—a team name—and the scroll would officially seal.

Instead, the six of them were crowded in the hallway outside the main office of Highveil Hall, arguing like roommates fighting over whose turn it was to do the dishes.

"I still think we should be Team Hexadecimal," Zeb said, goggles pushed high on his forehead. "It has structure. Symmetry. Power. It literally implies a six-unit team."

"Your name sounds like a calculator," Kennedy sighed, pinching the bridge of her nose.

"It sounds precise," Zeb shot back.

"It still sounds like a calculator," she mumbled again under her breath.

Tamlin adjusted his glasses and cleared his throat with ceremonial gravity. "If we're choosing names that carry history and symbolism, *The Loomers* is a clear winner. The loom is a weaver of fate. Threads. Destiny. A strong magical foundation."

"That sounds like a bunch of old grannies in a knitting circle," Zeb said.

“It does a little,” Pax murmured from his spot, leaning against the wall.

“I don’t care what we’re called,” Madi said, sitting cross-legged by the office door. “As long as it’s not something we’ll regret in the first five minutes.”

Kennedy nodded. “Same. But we need to decide now—the paperwork’s ready, we just need a name.”

Emric stared at the blank name line. On the other side of the glowing office door, Mrs. Atkinson was audibly grumbling about losing “the good scissors” again.

“Alright,” Emric said at last. “What about Team Vector?”

Everyone looked at him.

“It’s clean,” he said. “Abstract enough not to get us typecast. Sharp. Implies movement, force, trajectory—”

“I like it,” Madi said immediately.

“Better than a knitting circle or a calculator,” Kennedy added.

Tamlin frowned. “I’m not convinced.”

“I still think Hexadecimal would be cooler,” Zeb said stubbornly.

“How about Team Don’t Die?” Pax offered with complete sincerity.

Emric raised an eyebrow. “Vote?”

Hands went up:

- Zeb for *Hexadecimal*
- Tamlin for *The Loomers*
- Pax for *Team Don't Die*
- Emric, Madi, and Kennedy for *Team Vector*

"Three to one to one to one," Emric said, filling the line with quick strokes of the pen.

Golden light rippled across the scroll as the ink sealed and the paper stiffened.

The door swung open, and Team Vector entered. Inside, Mrs. Atkinson's desk was piled with floating scrolls and spinning lenses. She wasn't tall enough to see over it, but her voice carried cheerfully. "Is someone there?"

Emric stepped forward and handed her the scroll. It landed in a bronze tray and vanished with a *pop*. A moment later, the ceiling above shimmered to life—an enormous illusory canopy spinning slowly with dozens of glowing banners. One more blinked into existence: silver, marked with a crisp, angular emblem.

TEAM VECTOR

"Oh good, your roster sheet is perfect," Mrs. Atkinson said brightly. "You wouldn't believe how many teams—just today—had to rewrite theirs half a dozen times before they got accepted. That reminds me of the time I was going downtown to see if we could—"

"Thank you, Mrs. Atkinson," Principal Grimm's voice called from his office. "I'm sure these students are eager to get to class."

"Oh," Mrs. Atkinson replied with a genuine smile, "you're right, who am I to hold them up." She got up and walked into the principal's office. "That reminds me of the time I was held up by my mother before I could go to the prom, the boy who took me..."

Her voice trailed off as the newly accepted Team Vector exited the office and headed toward homeroom.

Tamlin's eyes went wide when he spotted the clock. "We need to hurry or we'll be late! That is unbecoming of the class peer leader."

He immediately started shove-running the group toward homeroom.

Tamlin enthusiastically herded them through the doorway just as the bell rang, shoving Emric forward like a sheepdog on a tight schedule.

Professor Beck was already leaning against his desk at the front of the room, a steaming mug in his hand and a bored look on his face that somehow still felt like he was daring someone to interrupt him.

"Ah," he said as they stumbled into their seats. "Team Vector, I presume? I saw your banner pop up in the tournament codex a couple of minutes ago. Congratulations—you've officially joined the chaos."

An excited ripple of chatter passed through the class.

Beck took a slow sip. "For the rest of you: over half of this class is now rostered. The rest of you have one month to form your teams and submit your names. I wouldn't wait until the last minute unless you're hoping to scrape together whatever strays are left once the good ones are gone."

A boy near the window raised his hand, practically bouncing in his chair. "Mr. Beck—my team's already formed as well. If another team wants to run some scrimmage matches, we're in!"

The ripple of chatter grew louder as students leaned toward their neighbors to whisper.

Beck smirked. "That's not a bad idea, Mr. Taylor. Scrimmages will make you better—or at least make you realize which of your teammates you should've cut sooner. Either way, I recommend it." He set his mug down with a *clink*. "Teams should try something before the tournament begins. Preferably something that doesn't end with me filling out paperwork."

When the bell rang, Emric jogged up to the boy Beck had called Mr. Taylor.

"Hey," Emric said. "My team and I want to take you up on your offer."

"Too easy, mate!" the boy grinned. "I'm Nick."

"Emric," he replied, shaking his hand. "Team Vector."

"We're the Fireballers," Nick said proudly. "I'll have a yarn with my mates and get back to you before the weekend."

The easy, rounded vowels and the *mates* made his Australian accent impossible to miss.

They tapped tags and exchanged info before heading their separate ways.

Emric found Tamlin, Pax, Madi, Kennedy, and Zeb waiting just outside the classroom door.

They were mid-discussion as Emric approached, and he rolled his eyes playfully when he heard Zeb insisting, "I'm still calling the team *Hexadecimal* in my mind."

Kennedy groaned and rolled her eyes, clearly annoyed.

"Good news," Emric said, holding up his mana tag. "I exchanged info with Nick—the Fireballers are in for a scrimmage. But if we're going to do this, we need a plan."

"The Fireballers?" Madi said, in the tone of someone who'd just stepped in something gross.

At the word *plan*, Zeb perked up. "Finally. Strategy talk."

"My place?" Emric suggested. "We can spread out, figure out roles, and see what our options are."

Zeb rubbed his hands together. "Good. I've got some things to show everyone—made some cool stuff for you guys."

Tamlin adjusted his glasses, clearly pleased. "Yes. Proper preparation before engagement."

Pax tilted his head. "Does your house have snacks?"

"It sure does," Emric replied. "I think my older brother just went shopping."

Emric's apartment felt one size too small with six teammates crammed into the living room, plus Nia curled up in the armchair like she'd claimed it for life.

Tamlin had taken the far end of the couch, straightening the books on the shelf. Pax had found a snack bowl left on the coffee table and sat cross-legged on the rug. Madi sprawled across the loveseat with a blanket, like it was movie night.

Kennedy lingered near the doorway, scanning the chaos with the expression of someone who'd just walked into a toddler's birthday party.

Zeb sat cross-legged on the floor near the coffee table, grinning to himself as he dug through his backpack—the soft clink of metal, the shimmer of crystals, and the occasional *thunk* of a tool hitting the floor.

"Alright," Emric said, unrolling the tournament rules scroll. "Pax, I think since you can—"

The front door swung open.

Kael stepped in, stopping dead when he saw the living room full of people. His gaze swept from the couch to the loveseat to Zeb's growing pile of parts on the rug.

"You didn't tell me you were bringing friends home," Kael said, voice sharp. "Do you know what that means?"

Emric and Nia looked at each other in a panic.

"Now I have to be a gracious host," Kael continued, like someone who'd just been handed a group project and knew he'd be doing all the work.

"Oh, sorry," Emric said, relieved that this was all that was the matter.

"Ugh," Kael grunted, disappearing into the kitchen. The sounds of cupboards opening and plates clattering followed.

Nia laughed. "Make sure you bring out the Glowbloom gummies."

"No moondrops?" Emric asked.

"I already ate them," Nia said, unapologetic.

From the kitchen came the sound of the icebox swinging open, followed by Kael's exasperated, "Unbelievable."

"Okay," Emric said, snapping the group's attention back.

Tamlin adjusted his glasses. "I would like to draw everyone's attention to rule seventeen. All items, weapons, and enchantments used in the tournament must be crafted by members of the team. No outside assistance allowed."

A slow grin spread across Zeb's face. "Good. Because that means the other teams don't stand a chance."

"Ugh," Kennedy muttered. "Now you're going to be even more insufferable."

Madi ignored them. "I can start enchanting our gear right away." Her eyes darted back and forth in a blur, like she was already designing custom pieces for each person in her head.

"Oh—" Madi's face lit up. "I can even make us matching jackets."

"Absolutely not," Kennedy said.

"C'mon, Kennedy!" Madi laughed. "We could at least look like a team."

Pax raised a pretzel, mouth full. "I vote for capes."

"No capes," Emric said instantly. "Haven't you ever seen *The Incredibles*? Plus, no one here is a superhero."

"Fine," Pax muttered in defeat, slumping back. The rest of the group snorted.

Kael returned with a charcuterie tray, a large bowl of gummies for Nia, and seven magically enchanted lemonades drifting in a neat line behind him. He set the tray down on the coffee table, and the lemonades floated one by one to each person. He gave Emric a look that very clearly said, *You owe me*, then disappeared into his room without another word.

"Alright," Emric said, pulling out a small conjuration scroll. He read it aloud, and with a *poof* of magical smoke, a whiteboard appeared in the room, complete with dry-erase markers and an eraser.

He spoke as he wrote: "Madi, enchantments. Zeb, tech. Kennedy, healing, and crowd control. Pax, close range. Tamlin, tactical oversight. I'll handle coordination and mid-range offense."

He turned to the group. "Any objections so far?"

Nobody answered right away. Zeb was scribbling in his notebook, eyes flicking between the whiteboard and the glowing pile of gadgets on the rug.

"I have some prototypes I've been working on," he said. "The one I wanted to show you today is a wrist-mountable mana reader, so you can get used to it before the scrimmage." He started digging through the pile, pulling out a handful of bracelets.

While he worked, Madi leaned forward. "I want to enchant my boots for speed. I can do that for everyone if you want, or you can pick something else. Just don't get too crazy—bigger enchants are more expensive. But if you got the orbs, then I'll do whatever you want."

Zeb finally gathered his things and stood. "Guys, check this out." He held up his bare wrist, then slid on a bracelet clearly too big for him. A moment later, it magically resized itself to fit perfectly, leaving his hand motions free. "This is a mana reader." He held the pose like he was waiting for fireworks.

Kennedy frowned. "Cool. What does it do?" Tamlin leaned in, curiosity piqued.

Zeb's smug smile deepened. "You place your mana tag in it, and it sends out an omnidirectional magical pulse that detects other mana tags within a set radius. Then it gives you information about that person."

Emric's eyes widened. "So… we can track the other team during a match? Where did you even get these?"

"I designed them myself," Zeb said, puffing up. "And not just tracking—they'll show domain, crest, potential output levels, and general health status."

Tamlin's brows rose. "That would be a significant tactical advantage. We could anticipate their movements and adjust our formation on the fly."

Kennedy's eyes narrowed—a flicker of genuine interest before she smothered it. "Does it tell us about our team too?"

"You better believe it, sister," Zeb said, leaning on the words like they made him cooler. "Same diagnostics for us, with fully customizable alert parameters for whatever thresholds you want monitored."

Kennedy's face went flat again. "Say that again. In English."

"He means," Emric cut in, "you can pick exactly what you want to track and get alerts for it. Ignore the other team entirely if you want, or just see where they are and what domain they specialize in." His grin spread. "Customizable intel."

"You took the words right out of my mouth," Zeb said, firing off a finger gun like they were perfectly in sync.

Madi's hand shot up. "I want one. If it means I can see someone coming before they even get close, I'm in. And I want it in silver. No—rose gold. Wait—silver with a rose-gold inlay."

Kennedy groaned. "It's not a fashion accessory, Madi."

Pax tilted his head. "Will it tell me if someone's invisible?"

"Sort of," Zeb admitted, his swagger dimming a fraction. "It can tell you someone's in front of you, but it won't break an invisibility enchantment. So you won't see them—you'll just know they're somewhere nearby."

"You can't," Tamlin said matter-of-factly, "but I can make a potion that will. You can drink it for temporary true sight, or throw it like a grenade to disperse an area-wide revealing mist."

Pax's eyes lit up. "Potion grenades? That sounds awesome."

"I have lots of potions we can use," Tamlin continued, adjusting his glasses. "Not just for drinking—some designed for strategic chaos on the field. Slippery oil slicks, smoke bombs, concussion bursts…"

Emric clapped his hands together. "Alright. We've got the tech, the potions, the enchantments, and the attitude. Now let's figure out how to make the Fireballers wish they'd never agreed to this."

Chapter 12

The Cloudrest Training Arena looked less like a gymnasium and more like a fragment of some otherworldly battlefield carved out and sealed indoors. Stone platforms floated at different heights, suspended over a shimmering floor of raw magic that occasionally flared like heat lightning. Tiered stands curved along the walls, already dotted with students who had come to watch.

"Feels like overkill for a practice match," Madi said, adjusting the strap of her satchel.

"That's because this isn't practice," Tamlin said brightly. "This is a live simulation. Every enchantment, every gadget, every decision you make will count. Tournament rules still apply, so think of it as the real thing."

Kennedy didn't even look up. "Yeah, but it's still just practice."

Tamlin slumped, his enthusiasm evaporating.

At the far end of the arena, two figures waited by a judge's platform. Professor Beck, sharp coat immaculate and wearing the expression of a man silently regretting his career choices, nursed a mug of whatever kept him from resigning. Beside him stood Professor Moss, waving cheerfully with… a hoof.

Not a hoof foot—those were surprisingly normal. Moss wore sandals, and his toes were perfectly human. But from the wrist down, his hands were glossy brown hooves, polished like he'd shined them that morning. He wiggled one in a wave, the motion somehow both friendly and deeply unsettling.

Madi blinked. "What's wrong with his hands?"

"Told you," Tamlin said to Emric. "He still can't figure it out."

Moss clopped his hooves together in greeting, speaking into a microphone. "Good morning, teams! It's a beautiful Saturday for simulated combat, bleeah."

Beck didn't look up. "Saturdays are for sleeping in, not early morning combat." He took another sip.

Nick and the rest of the Fireballers were already waiting in the arena—five players in matching crimson gear, their expressions ranging from confident to grim.

"See!" Madi declared to Kennedy. "Uniforms!"

Kennedy just rolled her eyes.

"Glad you made it," Nick called out, his accent carrying easily across the stone platforms. "When I booked this spot, I made sure we'd get the full works—minion waves, Keystones, towers, the lot. Five v five, just like the real deal."

"Sounds good to us," Emric said.

Nick shrugged. "We're only running five, so you've got the numbers on us."

"Not really," Emric said. "Zeb's not going in."

Nick's grin faltered. "Aw, you're kidding. I had plans for that one. He's the bloke who christened me Baron von Burp-a-Lot in front of the girl I was about to ask out. She laughed… then ghosted me. Haven't seen her since."

Zeb, sitting in the stands, shrank into his hoodie, trying to vanish.

"Yeah," Emric said, rubbing the back of his neck. "That's why he's not actually on the field."

Nick huffed a laugh and waved it off. "Righto, no hard feelings. You ready to get this show on the road?"

Beck gave a sharp whistle that sliced through the ambient hum of the arena. The sound bounced off the floating stone platforms, instantly quieting the scattered students in the stands.

"All right," he said, stepping forward. "You know the rules. The wards are up, but you can still get hurt—so don't be stupid." He gestured lazily to the walls, where faint silver glyphs shimmered. "These will also keep the spectators from becoming collateral damage."

"That's comforting," Madi said dryly.

Beck continued, voice flat as stone. "Since this is just a scrimmage, the mercenary camps won't be under faculty control. They'll function as stronger versions of the standard lane minions. Plan for that."

Professor Moss took the microphone with both hooves, clapping it against his polished forelegs like a toddler learning to hold a bottle. "For those who've never seen a simulated match before, here's how it works! Both teams start in their Keystone zones—their lovely, cozy home bases. Bleeah. Every thirty seconds, the arena will spawn minion waves: delightful little constructs whose only goal in life is to ruin yours. Defeating them allows for your team's minion waves to advance and take down their various tiers of defense, and will eventually give you access to their Keystone."

He rocked happily on his feet. "Destroy enemy towers to push the battle line forward toward their Keystone. First team to crack it wins the match, the glory, and maybe—maybe—the admiration of that special someone." His gaze slid across the arena like he knew exactly whose crushes he'd just exposed.

"Oh, and creativity's encouraged! Climb the towers, throw a minion, launch a pie—"

Beck took the mic mid-sentence. "There will be no pie throwing. We're monitoring all magic for safety violations and unsportsmanlike conduct. Play fair, or you're out."

Moss shrugged, unbothered.

"Teams, to your starting zones," Beck said, his voice carrying clean and firm. "Match begins in sixty seconds."

The platforms under Emric's team drifted apart, carrying them toward their glowing blue Keystone. Across the shimmering expanse, Nick and the Fireballers glided toward their crimson base.

Pax adjusted his mana reader on his wrist. "All right, here we go."

Kennedy cracked her knuckles. "I'll keep you alive if you don't do anything stupid."

From the stands, Zeb's voice crackled through their mana tags, smug and self-assured. "Relax. I've got eyes on the whole map. You'll know what's coming before they do."

The Keystone cores on each side flared to life, bathing the arena in blue and red light.

Somewhere above, a magical countdown began to echo: "Three… two… one…"

With a deep *shunk*, the floating platform dropped the last few feet, locking perfectly into a cutout in the arena floor. The impact sent a ripple of blue light across the edges—the signal that the match had officially begun.

Emric rolled his shoulders, glancing at each teammate in turn.

"All right," he said, voice steady. "Just like we practiced."

Kennedy and Madi peeled off toward the top lane, Pax and Tamlin headed for mid, and Emric broke away toward bottom—alone.

The moment his shoes crossed the glowing threshold, the scenery transformed. Smooth arena stone gave way to dense emerald moss, and towering trees rose on either side, their canopies so thick they swallowed the ceiling lights and drenched the lane in a deep green glow.

It felt alive—not just in the windless sway of the vines, but in the constant thrum of magic beneath his feet. Massive crystals jutted from the ground at odd angles, their facets glowing faintly like the heartbeat of the forest itself. Every so often, a pulse of arcane light rippled through them, sending a shiver through the mossy earth.

As Emric ran, faint glyphs flickered at the edges of his vision—Zeb's enhanced mana tag interface kicking in. Zeb's voice came through clearly in his ear.

"Okay, everyone," Zeb said. "I can only see what you see, so until you make contact, I'm blind. The second an enemy pops on your feed, I'll call it and send backup. Think of me as your map—but only the parts you've actually explored."

With a faint *whump*, the first wave of minions spawned behind Emric.

They looked like a child's drawing of a storm cloud brought to life—small, roiling masses of white vapor strapped with mismatched bits of armor: crude helmets, dented shoulder plates, and half-rusted chest plates floating over nothing. Their "faces" were narrow slits of light deep in the mist.

The front line—two bulkier clouds carrying battered shields—drifted forward with slow menace, armor clinking faintly. Behind them hovered three slimmer shapes with oversized crossbows that looked almost comically heavy. Between them floated a single mage construct, its "hands" swirling with currents of wind as it conjured spheres of crackling energy.

Emric picked up his pace, running ahead of his minions to intercept the enemy wave before it reached the midpoint.

His shoes thudded against the mossy lane as the forest began to thin. The deep green glow gave way to streaks of brighter light, and through the gap ahead, he caught sight of the first defense tower.

It wasn't a tower in the traditional sense—no bricks or battlements—but a jagged pillar of crystal wrapped in bands of floating metal, each piece etched with runes that pulsed in a slow rhythm. A massive lens hovered at its peak, rotating with lazy precision as it tracked movement in the lane below. Every so often, faint motes of energy bled from the surrounding air into the lens, building toward a tower shot.

The moment Emric's foot crossed the halfway point to the tower, the lens locked on him.

"Oh, that's not—"

A sharp *thunk* cracked the air, followed by a streak of condensed magic hurtling toward him. He tried to sidestep, but the shot was faster than he anticipated—only a heartbeat away from impact.

He slammed his hand against the buckle at his waist. A burst of blue light snapped outward, forming a hexagonal shield around him—**Arcane Bulwark**. The shot struck the barrier with a thunderclap, scattering shards of light across the lane before winking out entirely. The shield flickered once, then vanished, its five-second protection window spent in what felt like a single heartbeat. *Thanks, Madi*, he thought.

Dust and residual magic washed over him, and Emric dove out of the tower's firing range, lungs tight from the adrenaline spike.

By the time he straightened, his own minion wave had caught up—the shield-bearing vanguard drifting ahead, crossbow carriers lining up shots. The opposing wave appeared from the far end of the lane at almost the same moment, their armor clinking as they surged forward.

Without hesitation, the two sides collided. Shields slammed, bolts whistled, and the mage constructs began hurling their crackling orbs across the narrow forest lane.

A blur surged out of the emerald gloom—not a spell, but a weapon. A massive, spiked mace, spectral and oversized, whipped toward Emric's face, trailing ghostly vapor. He barely ducked in time. The head screamed past, stirring his hair before smashing into the mossy ground with a thunderous crack. A crater bloomed where it struck, rippling with dark blue spirit-light.

The mana tag reader flickered to life across Emric's vision:

Tyler Johnson – Crest of Essence

He had a full green health bar, full blue mana bar, but his stamina bar—orange—read 95%. Beneath that, it displayed: Rank – A – Sophomore.

A memory flickered in Emric's mind:

They were all sitting in his living room, staring at the conjured whiteboard. Zeb was talking.

"Technically, I didn't hack the academy's database. I just applied a little creative mana realignment to their security's flamewall."

"You hacked the school's system?!" Tamlin's voice had been incredulous.

"No, no," Zeb said, his smug grin firmly in place. "I just gave the login page a little... friendly encouragement. Let's just say I found a way to sync our tags with some very interesting records."

The memory blinked away as the mace's spectral chain rattled taut, and Tyler hauled the weapon back with one hand like it weighed nothing.

Emric's pulse spiked. A-rank. Top ten percent for his grade.

This wasn't going to be easy.

Tyler didn't waste time. With a sharp twist of his wrist, the spectral chain rattled, and the massive mace blurred through the air again, carving a brutal arc meant to crush Emric flat.

Emric dove sideways just in time, shoes skidding across moss slick with arcane dew. The mace slammed down where he'd been a second before, sending a shockwave through the ground that rattled his teeth.

He thrust out a palm, muttering the incantation. A streak of blue-violet light lanced across the lane. The Arcane Blast hit Tyler square in the chest—only to pass straight through him. The figure dissolved like smoke.

Spectral afterimage, Emric realized too late.

Three more Tylers flickered into being—one perched in the branches above, the others fanning out across the lane.

His mana tag interface adjusted automatically, reading all four Tylers with identical data. No differences. No giveaways. Even with Zeb's upgrades, the system couldn't tell an afterimage from the real thing.

The Tyler in the tree raised a spectral bow strung with dark-blue spirit light. The arrow loosed with a whisper.

Emric slapped his buckle. Instead of a shield, a bright red alert seared across his vision:

WARNING: Arcane Bulwark cooldown – 2:45 remaining

His chest tightened. That was only fifteen seconds ago...

The arrow slammed into his shoulder, bursting in a flare of ghostlight. The energy dissipated, but the pain did not—hot and sharp, ripping through his nerves and nearly buckling his knees.

Emric staggered back, breath hissing between his teeth. His health indicator dropped by a third and turned yellow. The hit wasn't lethal, but the jolt was brutal enough to shake him. *If this was "safe," he didn't want to imagine what the tournament would be like without the safety wards.*

The battle moved fast, and one mistake was already costing him.

The first Tyler reappeared between the other two on the ground.

All four Tylers closed in, spectral chains rattling as the massive mace swept overhead, while the one in the tree nocked another arrow.

Emric's mana tag kept flashing the same readout for every copy, mocking him.

His breath came fast, panic clawing at the edges of his focus. He couldn't keep dodging forever.

Think. They're illusions. Only one is real.

He forced himself to look past the glowing weapons, past the haze of spirit-light. That's when he saw it—only one Tyler actually touched the world around him. The moss bent under his boots. Leaves shifted at his passing. Dust curled up where his mace dragged. The others left nothing.

“There you are,” Emric muttered.

His gut twisted. He still didn’t know if the fake weapons were harmless; the arrow earlier sure hadn’t felt fake. He couldn’t risk guessing wrong.

The Tyler to his right lunged, mace whistling on its chain. Emric pivoted, thrust both hands forward, and an Arcane Blast ripped through the illusion. It burst like smoke—gone.

But the real Tyler was already winding up for the next swing.

Emric’s first instinct was to retreat, to throw himself backward out of range—

Get in close. Don’t run.

The whisper again, clearer this time—deep, steady, almost familiar. The cadence tugged at something in him, like a half-remembered lullaby or an old story told at his bedside. It shouldn’t have been possible, but he could almost place it.

It steadied his panic in a way that felt unnatural, and before he realized it, his body obeyed.

He darted forward, slipping inside the arc of the chain. His pulse thundered in his ears. Insane—utterly insane—listening to a voice in his head. But here he was, in the perfect spot for an Arcane Explosion.

He got right up to the real Tyler's face and shoved both hands outward.

A shockwave of blue-violet force erupted from his core, rolling out in every direction. The moss flattened. Branches rattled overhead. Raw arcane light tore through the lane in a blast like a thunderclap.

Tyler took the full brunt of the spell at point-blank range. It hit like a freight train, hurling him backward, chain whipping loose as the mace went clattering into the moss and vanished in sparks of green mana shards.

Tyler's health bar nosedived, plunging straight into red.

Emric froze, chest heaving. He'd expected pushback, but not this. The damage was brutal—far more than he thought he could dish out. *I guess they call it "explosion" for a reason*, he thought numbly.

But Tyler was still standing. Staggered, sleeve shredded, and arm scorched with arcane burns—but standing. His eyes locked onto Emric, and the chain reformed in his grip.

Emric swallowed hard. This wasn't over yet.

Tyler narrowed his eyes, raising the mace handle skyward. With a pulse of green energy, the weapon reformed, dripping wisps of ghostlight—heavier, meaner than before.

"Seriously?" Emric muttered, tightening his stance, fingers flexing.

Tyler's health was low, but that only made him more dangerous—a cornered fighter with nothing left to lose.

The Fireballer lunged, swinging the mace in a brutal horizontal sweep meant to crush Emric against the trunk of a towering tree.

The swing was clumsy, slowed by his injuries, but still deadly. Emric ducked, the wind of the weapon grazing his hair. He snapped off an Arcane Blast, but Tyler twisted, letting it sear past. The counter was immediate: the chain snapped taut, yanking the mace around midair. It came screaming back like a meteor.

"Emric, on your left!" Zeb's voice cut through his mana tag.

He pivoted—but too late. The chain lashed across his side, detonating with raw force. Pain ripped through his ribs, vision blurring as his health bar plunged deep into the red.

He staggered, catching himself on shaky feet, the entire left side of his body burning with ghostfire agony.

Tyler reeled the mace back in, eyes locked on him with grim determination. He wasn't just surviving anymore—he was winning.

Tyler came down like a hurricane, chain rattling as the mace whipped in savage arcs. Each swing was heavier, faster, fueled by sheer willpower. The air itself seemed to howl with every pass, ghostfire sparking against the green plant life.

Emric stood his ground, teeth gritted. Every breath was agony. His vision blurred and swam.

He braced, raw mana prickling across his fingertips. He couldn't rely on another bulwark yet—the cooldown timer still blinked at him, unforgiving. His only shot was timing.

He steadied himself, eyes darting—not at the mace, not at the chain, but at Tyler's stance. His boots pressed into the moss, weight shifting with each swing. The afterimages were gone now; Tyler seemed to be focusing all his energy on maintaining the spectral mace rather than his doppelganger trick.

Come on, Emric thought. *Just one more.*

Tyler, unknowingly obliging, snarled as he heaved the mace overhead for a crushing vertical strike. The weapon glowed with spirit energy, every ounce of his essence pouring into it.

Emric's heart pounded, the air shuddered. He saw the swing coming. He didn't dodge—he stepped in again.

Tyler's eyes narrowed—he was expecting Emric to rush him. With a vicious jerk, he snapped the chain taut. The mace whipped back with terrifying speed, a green comet screaming for Emric's skull.

But instead of charging, Emric dropped flat. His body slammed into the moss, chest scraping the ground as the mace roared overhead—then reversed course.

Too late, Tyler realized. His own mace had no loyalty.

The spectral mace slammed into him full force, crushing through his guard in an eruption of ghostlight. His body staggered backward, armor cracking with arcs of blue-green energy as Tyler vanished from the playing field.

For a moment, silence hung in the lane—until the clash of another minion wave shattered it.

Oh no. Had he just—?

"Ladies and gentlemen! Bleeaah!" Professor Moss's voice boomed cheerfully through the loudspeakers. "We have our first knockout of the match! Tyler Johnson will respawn in thirty seconds."

Emric blinked, chest heaving. *Respawn. Right. Not dead.*

Across the battlefield, inside a booth of shimmering light at the crimson Keystone, Tyler's body reformed piece by piece, whole and unscathed. He was already cracking his neck and rolling his shoulders, waiting for the timer to drop so he could storm back onto the field.

Emric dragged a hand down his face, exhaling hard. Relief flooded through him, quickly replaced by the gnawing realization—

He'd won the first duel of the match.

And that was just the opening move.

Chapter 13

Emric stood there, gazing up at the tower. After that fight with Tyler, taking it down by himself with barely a sliver of health seemed impossible.

He was still trying to piece together a plan when Zeb's voice cut in through his mana tag.

"Don't just stand there, Vale! You're deep in the red—if one of them rotates down, you're toast! Get back to the Keystone—it'll heal you."

Emric gritted his teeth. "Are you sure?"

Even without seeing him, Emric could hear Zeb's eye roll.

"Yes, dummy! Didn't you read the rulebook?"

"There's a rulebook?" Emric shot back, sarcasm sharp.

"Unbelievable. Just go!" Zeb barked.

Emric started jogging, one arm wrapped over his ribs. He'd barely made it five steps before Zeb's voice snapped again.

"What are you doing? You don't have to run! Just tap your crest!"

Emric blinked. "My crest? What's that supposed to—"

Zeb groaned like a teacher on his last nerve.

"Put your finger on it, hold for five seconds, and don't move. The arena's enchanted to recall you to base and restore everything—health, mana, stamina, the works."

Emric stared down at the polished crest. His hand hovered uncertainly.

"You seriously need to read that rulebook, man," Zeb muttered.

Emric pressed the crest. It flared to life. Light spiraled up from his shoes, weaving runes around his body like a glowing cocoon. The battlefield shimmered, edges bending as if he were sinking underwater.

A blink later, the moss and trees were gone. Emric stood in the Keystone chamber, bathed in a cool blue glow. His health bar shot back to full, mana and stamina bars ticking upward like fast-forwarded gauges.

Emric let out a shaky exhale. "...Okay. That's incredible."

The glow around him dimmed as the Keystone chamber came into focus. For a moment, Emric just stood there, letting the relief sink in. No pain. No limp. No burning in his ribs.

Then his mana tag chimed.

A translucent 3D map unfolded in the air before him, like a floating tabletop game board. Blue dots pulsed where his teammates were scattered across the lanes, red dots showing the Fireballers pressing in. He counted only four enemy markers—three moving on the map, and Tyler still in the respawn chamber at the crimson base.

So he could only see what his team's vision covered.

Every tower glowed like a beacon, and minions swarmed along the glowing lanes in neat, colliding waves. All of that, he knew, was standard. Every player had this view from their respective Keystones.

But as his gaze lingered on a blue dot, extra data spilled out beside it: health, mana, and stamina bars.

Emric blinked. "Wait… I can see their stats?"

Zeb's voice crackled in his ear, smug as ever. "Yup. Everyone else? They just get dots. You get the full picture."

Emric let out a short laugh. "So, you hacked my map."

"Not hacked," Zeb said. "Enhanced."

His eyes swept over the board again. Bottom lane: Tamlin had rotated down to cover for him, stamina solid and pressure steady against the tower. Mid: Pax's health and stamina were both scraping yellow, but Kennedy's mana was dropping in sync with his bar climbing back up—she was keeping him alive.

Top lane: Madi.

Her lone marker pulsed frantically as two red dots closed in. Her mana bar was already thin, her stamina flashing orange.

Then, as Emric watched, her health ticked down another notch.

His stomach dropped. She was cornered.

Zeb's voice cut in sharply. "Vale, stop spectating and move! If they drop Madi, they'll collapse on that tower in seconds. Cut through the jungle—you'll hit them before they close the push."

The map rotated automatically, a pulsing trail tracing the shortest route.

Emric flexed his hands, mana prickling hot and ready. "Guess that rulebook you keep talking about doesn't have a chapter on cheat codes."

Zeb's laugh buzzed through the channel. "Buddy, I *am* the cheat code."

Emric rolled his eyes. Zeb was such a dork.

The projection faded as the Keystone gates pulsed open. Emric sprinted out, shoes hammering against stone, and veered toward the jungle trail.

The canopy broke ahead, spilling green light across the lane. Emric burst from the tree line just as Madi staggered back, her boots grinding furrows into the moss.

Two Fireballers pressed her hard. Emric focused on the pair; they looked like brothers.

The projection shimmered, numbers sliding into focus above their heads.

Collin Newell – Crest of Chain

Chase Newell – Crest of Veil

Both brothers were rank B, and Madi had worn them down—their health bars glowing yellow, stamina flickering orange.

Madi's own bars bled red-orange, her chest heaving as she raised another glyph. Even drained, she held her ground.

Collin carried himself like he owned the field—chin high, a cocky tilt in his stance—while Chase hung a step back, expression unreadable.

Collin grinned and flicked his wrist. A contract card spun out of nowhere, chains sparking across its surface. He slammed it into the air, the sigil flaring until it grew larger than he was. Chains rattled as a shape tore through.

A massive Utahraptor hit the moss with a bone-shaking thud, feathers bristling like quills, talons gleaming. Its eyes burned with chainlight as it threw back its head and screeched, the sound rattling Emric's teeth.

"Meet Zeke!" Collin bellowed.

The ground itself seemed to quake as the beast lunged forward, teeth bared.

Before Emric could react, Chase raised his weapon—a slim, rune-stamped gun humming with Veil-light. He aimed it—not at Emric, not at Madi—but at Zeke.

Emric's stomach lurched. *What the hell is he doing?*

A shot cracked, sharp and metallic. Light slammed into Zeke's side. The raptor glowed, staggered—then split.

One blinding chain of light became two. Then three.

The glow shattered.

Standing in the lane were not one, but three Utahraptors—every feather, every fang, every bloodthirsty gleam in their eyes identical.

All three Zekes turned as one, chains glowing at their throats. Then they charged.

All three screeched in unison, the sound splitting the air like tearing metal. Claws gouged moss. Jaws snapped.

Madi's chest rose and fell in sharp bursts, sweat streaking her brow. Then—against all odds—she grinned.

She leveled her staff. Runes blazed down the wood, flaring with sharp, rhythmic pulses.

Chains of violet light snapped outward, hooking into each raptor's chest. The beasts froze mid-step, eyes flickering as though their wills had been hijacked.

Emric's mana tag shimmered into view:

Enthusiastic Self-Discipline

Target is compelled to redirect aggression inward. Duration: 6 seconds. Bypasses most resistance due to self-referential paradox.

Emric blinked. *Wait... what?*

The Zekes lurched violently. One slashed its own chest with hooked claws. Another whipped its head sideways, teeth sinking into its flank. The third swung its tail like a club, cracking itself across the ribs.

They tore into themselves in a grotesque, synchronized frenzy.

Emric's gut clenched. *That's my window.*

He darted forward, slipping inside their chaos. Mana surged hot through his veins, his core crackling like thunder. The air boomed.

Arcane Explosion ripped out from him in a dome of violet-white light, flattening grass, shaking branches. The shockwave crashed into the trio of raptors, lifting them clean off their claws and hurling them back in a storm of shredded feathers.

They hit the moss with concussive thuds, the summons bursting apart in showers of chainlight and dissipating mana.

Emric staggered upright, chest heaving, vision swimming with sparks.

Beside him, Madi lowered her staff just a fraction, lips quirking into a breathless grin. "Well," she said between gulps of air, "that's one way to deal with a pack of dinosaurs."

Emric barked out a laugh. "Please tell me that spell wasn't literally called *Make the Giant Lizards Punch Themselves.*"

Madi's grin widened, teeth flashing. "Close enough."

But across the lane, Collin was already sliding another glowing card between his fingers, his smirk sharp as a blade. Chase leveled that strange gun, its runes crackling with fresh light.

Emric swallowed hard, flexing his hands as mana prickled hot again. "Round two," he muttered.

But before either brother could make a move, Madi unclasped a thin silver bracelet from her wrist and, with a flick of her hand, hurled it across the lane. It bounced off the helmet of a charging minion and rolled to a silent stop between the brothers.

Collin and Chase braced, waiting for an explosion or some hidden trick. Nothing happened.

Confused, they glanced down at the bracelet, then back up at her.

Silence.

Collin barked out a laugh. "Seriously? Well done..."

Chase snorted, cocking his gun. "Nice throw, though."

Collin lifted his foot, bracing to toss his next card like a pitcher on the mound—

And froze mid-step. His smirk collapsed into confusion as his leg twitched, then kicked out at an odd angle. His arms flailed, chest jerking.

"What the—?" Collin stomped—not with aggression, but rhythm. His shoulders popped. His head snapped side to side.

"Collin?" Chase asked, lowering his gun.

Then Chase began to twitch as well. His free hand shot up, elbow jerking. His knees bent and locked, torso rolling in sharp, unnatural motions. He started to pop and lock like a puppet on invisible strings.

Emric blinked, wide-eyed. "Are they… dancing?"

Beside him, Madi slipped off another bracelet. This one hung suspended in mid-air, pulsing once before music blasted out across the lane.

Never gonna give you up, never gonna let you down—

Rick Astley's voice boomed through the top lane like a battle anthem.

"What is going on in top lane?" Zeb's voice came in over their mana tags, half panicked, half disbelieving.

Collin's arms flailed as his legs stomped out a beat, his movements jerky but undeniably rhythmic. Chase mirrored him a second later, body rolling in sync like invisible strings yanked them both into a battle they hadn't signed up for.

"Ah, crap—!" Collin yelled, his voice breaking between pops of his shoulders. His free hand spasmed against his Crest. Chase's did the same, both of them slapping down as if the arena itself had seized control.

The Crests pulsed once. Then again.

Light flared upward, weaving into tight spirals that wrapped their twitching bodies like cocoons.

Both brothers danced wide-eyed as recognition hit them at the same time. "No, no, no—!" Collin's protest warped as the recall dragged him under. Chase's face stayed stoic, though even his head bobbed to the rhythm until the light swallowed them both.

And then—gone. Nothing left but moss, and Rick Astley echoing across top lane.

Emric exhaled hard, lowering his hands. "I did not expect that at all."

Madi smirked, brushing hair from her face. "They'll be back soon enough. Let's make it hurt in the meantime."

Her staff tapped against the mossy floor. A ripple of bright green light surged outward, collapsing to Emric's feet before flooding into his chest.

His mana tag shimmered information only he could see:

Courageous Accord

Next offense spell cast deals x4 damage. Doesn't work against opposing team's Keystone. Cooldown: 10 minutes.

Emric blinked. *Ten minutes? That's once, maybe twice a match.*

Warmth surged through his limbs—steadier than adrenaline, sharper than panic. He turned to the looming tower, focus locking in tight. Their minion wave was already pressing forward—perfect cover.

"All right then," he muttered, planting his stance.

He thrust out his hand.

Arcane Blast detonated like a thunderclap, violet-white force smashing into the runed pillar. Cracks spiderwebbed instantly, glyphs stuttering, the great lens at the peak glowing wildly before bursting apart in a rain of shattered light.

The entire tower groaned, then came down in a roaring cascade of crystal shards and drifting mana dust. The ground quaked with the collapse, a wave of hot air rolling through the lane. From the stands above, cheers finally erupted—loud and chaotic.

"Team Vector has successfully taken down top lane's tower. Well done," Beck's dry voice cut in over the PA, flat as ever.

Chapter 14

The top lane tower still smoldered behind them, shards of mana glass hissing into vapor. Emric jogged to catch up with Madi. Her windblown hair framed bright eyes, and a glint of sweat traced her cheekbone.

She looked—alive in a way he couldn't explain.

He grinned. "That was the most impressive Rickroll I've ever seen."

Madi laughed and gave a tired shrug. "They were never gonna give us up."

Zeb's voice crackled through the mana tags, excited and breathless. "Okay, okay—officially in the lead! Full tower down, one confirmed KO. Pfff, I'm making you guys look so good out there."

Tamlin followed immediately, clipped and focused. "Top push is over. Regroup. Pax needs support mid. Rotate now while their top flank is resetting."

Emric exhaled, still catching his breath. "Copy. We're coming, Pax."

Pax grunted in response.

Emric darted down the lane, hopping over broken roots and mana-scorched stone. It took him a second to realize—Madi wasn't with him.

He turned back. She was already cutting deeper into the top lane, fast and low.

"Wait, you're not coming mid?" he called.

"I'll flank from the jungle once you're in," Madi replied over the tag. "You're faster—I'll catch up."

Emric double-checked his belt. His Arcane Bulwark cooldown had reset, which made him feel a little safer. But something still clawed at his nerves.

"Just… watch your back," he called after her.

Over her shoulder, she shouted, "Watch your face."

Zeb laughed in his ear. Emric rolled his eyes.

Tamlin arrived in mid just as Emric cut in from the opposite side. They gave each other a short nod and turned their attention forward.

Pax stood near the edge of the lane, towering in full golem form—his body plated in rock and dark earth, shoulders like cliff walls. His massive arms shielded Kennedy, who hovered behind him, green forest magic swirling around her hands as she cast regeneration spells across his back.

Across from them were Nick and Tyler.

Or—Tylers, plural. The battlefield shimmered with identical duplicates of Tyler's illusion clones, each wielding spectral weapons. Nick stood beside them, flanked by two small fire elementals that hissed and crackled with burning eyes.

They weren't trying to overpower Pax with strength—they were going for numbers, illusions, distraction. And it was working. Pax was starting to stagger. His plates had cracked in two places, and Kennedy's magic pulsed harder to keep up.

Tamlin planted his boots on the moss, sliding to a stop. Emric halted beside him.

"If we hit now," Tamlin said, voice tight, "we can push them back and give Pax some breathing room."

Emric nodded. "You signal Pax. I'll hit the backline."

Zeb's voice buzzed through the tags. "Heads up—twenty seconds, maybe less, before their fifth joins mid. Got a red blip leaving bot lane and cutting through jungle. Can't track who it is yet."

"I still haven't seen their support," Tamlin muttered, fingers tightening around a small flask. "Whoever it is, they've been invisible this whole match."

Emric blinked. "You think they're cloaked support? Hiding while feeding buffs while stealthed?"

"Wouldn't surprise me," Tamlin muttered.

He pulled a vial from his pouch, the liquid inside glowing with shifting violet fog. "If we're gonna move—now's the time. Before they outflank us."

Tamlin hurled the vial.

It exploded mid-air with a sharp pop, the fog inside coalescing into slick frost across the moss. One of the Tylers—this one wielding a two-handed ghostlight axe—skidded off balance and stumbled straight into a colossal backhand from Pax.

The illusion dispersed instantly, vaporizing into shards of light.

Kennedy moved just enough to cast a chain heal—green threads whipped from her hands to Pax's shoulder, knitting cracked stone back together.

Emric sprinted forward, clearing the tower's range, arcane mana already crackling between his fingertips.

He raised his hand and let loose a razor-clean Arcane Blast.

It struck the real Tyler mid-back—just as he was drawing a bow of spiritlight. The conjured weapon exploded in his hands with a flash of ghostfire. Emric didn't realize it until after the shot fizzled, but that had been a ghostbomb arrow.

He'd just interrupted something very bad.

"Nice!" Zeb whooped. "That was—wait. Hold up."

The excitement vanished from his voice.

Emric's mana tag blinked. A flicker—small, faint—moving along the treeline.

"Left flank," Zeb said. "I think I saw something on the map."

Emric spun, eyes scanning the misted treeline.

There.

The leaves shimmered—just for a second. Like light bending wrong. A warped patch of air, heatless and silent.

Kennedy screamed in pain.

Emric turned just in time to see her dissolve in a burst of white-blue light—her body vanishing as the respawn enchantment triggered. No warning. No attack animation. Just gone.

She was gone.

"Kennedy!" Pax roared, the sound shaking the stones beneath them.

Madi's voice cut in, breathless and urgent. "What happened?! I'm almost there."

Emric's chest tightened. He hadn't seen the spell. No glyph. No gesture. Just that shimmer.

Tamlin's voice was clipped and grim. "Stealth caster. Support's using Veil and Confusion. They took her out. She's gone for at least thirty."

"Pax, fall back!" Emric shouted. "Your healer's gone—!"

But Pax was already roaring, fists raised, charging like a living avalanche.

"Crap! Too late," Emric muttered. "We're in it now."

Pax's stone-plated feet cracked the lane as he thundered forward, the rage in his roar echoing across the arena. Each step left shallow craters in the mossy stone.

Nick turned tail instantly, scrambling behind his fire elementals. The remaining Tyler clone launched a barrage of phantom daggers, hoping to slow Pax's charge, like trying to stop a landslide by asking it nicely.

Emric veered toward Pax's right, breath tight and senses straining. Too easy. Too quiet.

Zeb's voice crackled through the mana tag, heavy with static. "Trying to reestablish—ghht—something's interrupting—" Then silence.

"Veil field," Tamlin muttered. "They're blanketing this whole part of the arena."

Emric's heart lurched. They'd run full speed into a trap.

"Can we dispel it?" he shouted, scanning the jungle's edge.

"Not without knowing where it's being channeled from," Tamlin snapped, frustration in his voice. He knew it too; they were caught.

Tamlin flicked him a small red vial.

Then a flicker. Barely visible.

Emric didn't think. He spun and fired.

A sharp Arcane Blast tore through the mist with a heavy *whoosh* and hit nothing but air.

Then a voice, soft, right behind his ear.

“Close. But you missed.”

He whipped around. No one there.

Pax slammed both fists down in a thunderclap, shattering two of Nick’s summoned elementals. Their bodies scattered into smoke and ash, vanishing as if reality had rejected them. Nick stumbled, forced to retreat again.

But Pax didn’t stop.

“Pax!” Emric shouted. “Back! You don’t have a healer. Fall back!”

Too late.

A glyph ignited beneath Pax’s feet, red and angular, like thorned chains snapping out of the stone, and detonated upward in a twisting spiral. He was yanked into the air, body locked mid-motion, stone armor cracking across his shoulder.

He hit the ground like a meteor, carving a crater into the moss. His health bar plunged almost to empty.

Tamlin hurled a vial past him. A burst of luminous blue slowed Nick’s retreat just long enough for Emric to smash the red vial against Pax’s chestplate. It hissed, seeping into his stone form as his health began to crawl upward, painfully slow.

Then Madi dropped from the treeline.

A blur of sigils and starlight, she landed beside Pax, hand snapping forward. A glowing disc whirled from her palm, struck Nick's barrier, and detonated, staggering him back.

"Get Pax up!" she shouted. "I've got cover!"

But even as she spoke, Emric felt it again.

The shimmer.

To the left.

"No, Madi!" he yelled.

She didn't scream.

The Veil Hex flared beneath her, purple-black tendrils lashing up her legs and dragging her down through the stone. She fought it long enough to glance at Emric, sharp and unspoken, before gasping, "Sorry, guys," and vanishing in a burst of recall light. KO'd.

Emric's stomach dropped. The world seemed to tilt. The space where she'd stood was empty, his pulse pounding in his ears.

That was twice now. And it had been her.

"What's going on?" Pax groaned, pushing himself upright.

"We walked into a trap!" Emric snapped, eyes fixed on the ground where Madi had been.

Pax's jaw tightened. "My bad."

Emric swallowed hard. "We'll talk about it later."

Another shimmer.

This time, right in front of him.

The chill hit first, displacement magic crawling along his skin. Then a shape flickered into view, ten feet away. A half-masked face, pale lips curved into a knowing smirk.

The Veil mage.

Emric raised his hand, palm glowing, and fired an Arcane Blast straight through her head.

It passed like smoke.

The voice brushed his ear again, low and amused. "Missed again."

"Show yourself!" Emric barked.

"Why?" she asked. "You're exactly where I want you."

A shadow dart sliced across Emric's cheek, leaving a burning line of blood before dissolving into mist.

Her attacks weren't lethal, just cruel reminders that she was in control. And she was enjoying every second.

Emric's breath came too fast, shallow, and ragged. He forced his stance lower, mana thrumming in his palms, but his eyes betrayed him. They flicked back to the empty space where Madi had vanished.

Kennedy had gone down earlier, and that sucked, yes. But this… this was different.

It rattled him. Too much.

His chest ached, not fear for a teammate but something sharper. Personal. He clenched his jaw hard. *Not now. Later. I'll deal with this later.*

"Wake up, Emric!" Tamlin barked.

Emric snapped back as Tamlin yanked a small glass bottle from his belt.

"Incoming!" Tamlin shouted.

He pitched the vial overhand. It burst between Tyler and Nick, spilling into a luminous sludge that spread like a living blob, coating everything it touched in sticky crystalline slime. The Fireballers never saw it coming.

Pax pushed himself upright, stone shoulders grinding back into place as his body swelled toward full golem form.

Tyler's remaining clone slammed shoulder-first into the goo and was swallowed whole. To his team's shock, the Veil mage was caught mid-flicker, clipped by the spreading wave. The outline of her cloaked body rippled into view as the goo hardened into jagged crystal.

Three of them, trapped.

"NOW, PAX!" Tamlin shouted.

Pax surged forward, massive fists raised, and brought them down in a hammerblow that made the arena quake.

The crystal prison shattered—and so did the three Fireballers. Light burst outward as all three were ripped from the field, sent screaming back to the respawn chamber.

Zeb whooped in Emric's ear, his voice finally clear now that the Veil mage's interference had been broken.

But Emric didn't celebrate. His mind replayed the flicker of starlight sigils, the way Madi's eyes had met his before she was pulled under. He shook it off and forced himself to focus on the lane.

That's when it all went to crap.

The following events happened within one second of Pax's hammerblow against the enemy team.

A rune flared beneath Pax's massive foot, bright and intricate, spiraling outward like a blooming flower of light.

A second rune flared behind Tamlin. His glasses caught the reflection; he turned, and a star-blazoned sigil burned at his back.

The two sigils folded together and snapped shut like a gigantic set of jaws.

Both Pax and Tamlin were swallowed by a vertical burst of crimson light, their bodies stiffening mid-motion before vanishing in twin flashes. KO'd.

The lane fell silent.

Emric stood frozen, lungs straining, staring at the empty space where his teammates had been a heartbeat earlier.

Three Fireballers gone. Two teammates gone.

Nothing moved. Nothing breathed.

Except his heartbeat—still pounding, refusing to calm. Why wasn't his heart calming? Something was wrong.

Then came the sound of crystal breaking apart.

From within the splintered shell of Tamlin's goo bomb, a shadow stirred. A figure slipped through the jagged shards like a ghost passing through a wall.

The Veil mage.

Her cloak hung in tatters from Pax's hammerblow, but her eyes gleamed cold and unshaken beneath her half-mask.

"You've got to be kidding me," Emric said quietly.

She stepped forward, dragging the tip of one finger along the crystalline residue as if testing the texture. The goo hissed and evaporated at her touch.

"You thought I'd be gone with the others?" she said, voice lit with amusement. "You're so adorable."

Emric's eyebrow shot up, unsure whether to be confused, offended, or oddly flattered.

It was just him.

Her.

And the space between them.

Then she tilted her head, mask glinting. "Tell you what, Emric. If you surrender now, I'll let you take me on a date."

His brain short-circuited. His eyes went wide, and heat slammed into his face so fast it made his ears burn. A date? Here? Now? Was she serious? Was this a trick? Or was she just trying to throw him off his game?

Judging by the smirk tugging at her lips, the answer was yes—to all of it.

He wasn't mad about the idea. In fact, he kind of liked it. He'd never had a girl be into him bef—

That's when he heard the whisper again.

Duck!

Emric didn't think. He dropped to one knee just as a blade of shadow hissed through the air where his head had been. The air shimmered, her form flickering into view for an instant before sliding back into distortion.

His chest heaved, adrenaline spiking. If he hadn't listened to the whisper again, he'd be KO'd—just like with Tyler.

The mage's sweet laughter drifted through the mist. "Quick reflexes. I like that."

Emric tightened his fist, jaw set. This time, he could almost place the whisper. Somewhere in his mind, rattling just out of reach, he knew that voice. But he couldn't pin it down.

But that was for another time. He couldn't afford another distraction—not when it had nearly cost his team another KO.

The air shimmered again.

Her laugh slid around him, circling and impossible to place. "That focus looks good on you. Let's see how long you can keep it up."

Shadows snapped across the lane, blades darting in from three angles at once. Emric slammed his buckler. Arcane Bulwark flared from his core in a wave of translucent energy, the shield snapping outward to catch the blades.

The barrier vanished as quickly as it came. She shimmered away again.

He spun a full circle, mana sparking in his palms, sweat beading down his temple. *Where? Where—?*

And then—

Now. Drop low.

The whisper sliced through his panic.

Emric dropped flat, palms hitting the mossy floor, just as her blade whistled over his head. For a split second, her veil faltered—her form flickering into view directly above him.

Instinct took over. He thrust both hands upward.

A raw Arcane Explosion tore out of him, bursting through the air point-blank.

She was sent flying, trailing violet-blue mana threads, her cloak shredded, her half-mask shattered. For the first time, her eyes widened—not amused, but shocked. She hit the moss and slid to a stop on her back.

Emric scrambled to his feet, chest heaving. His body shook from the jolt of near-death adrenaline and the surge of arcane power that had just exploded out of him.

But he'd landed a hit.

A real hit.

And it hadn't been luck.

He focused on her, and his mana tag flashed across his vision:

Shaylee Rose – Crest of Veil

Rank: S

His breath caught. S-rank? Holy crap, no wonder she'd been toying with him.

Her health bar hovered deep in the red, pulsing faintly, while her mana and stamina were still halfway full.

Emric swallowed hard. That wasn't a good sign. Not at all. He'd barely gotten in one solid hit—a strong hit—but it was still a single hit. And she still had enough juice left to bury him three times before his body was sent to the respawn location.

Shaylee Rose slowly got to her feet, brushing the broken pieces of her mask from her shoulder as if the blast had only been an inconvenience. Her smile returned—thinner now, edged with irritation.

"Well," she said softly, "you're full of surprises."

Emric clenched his fists, trying to keep his knees from shaking. He glanced at his tag's readout again. **S-rank.** How was he supposed to win this?

"Emric!" Zeb's voice cut through the mana link, jittery, but at least it was finally clear this time. "Good news—Kennedy's almost to your position. She got held up, stopping a minion wave from destroying our tower, but she's on the move again. Madi just respawned. Tamlin and Pax are both seven seconds out. If you can hold a little longer, you'll have backup."

Relief flooded his chest—then curdled instantly into panic.

If his team was regrouping, so was hers.

His gut twisted. The Fireballers would be converging on mid at the same time. He wasn't staring down a duel. He was staring down a countdown.

He looked back at Shaylee. Her health bar still glowed red, low but not gone. Her mana and stamina were—annoyingly—slowly creeping upward. Her stance stayed loose, calm—like a predator waiting for the right second to strike.

She called out, her voice teasing. "The offer's still on the table. I like Chinese food."

If he waited—if he tried to stall—her reinforcements would reach her first. Then she'd melt back into the shadows, untouchable.

There was only one choice.

He had to finish it. Right now. One-on-one.

Shaylee seemed to know it too. Her smirk deepened, and she vanished. The veil snapped over her again, and suddenly the air came alive with blades of shadow.

Emric dodged, ducked, dipped, dived, and dodged again, his stamina burning fast. Every strike and dodge forced him back another step. *He couldn't win a war of attrition.*

Focus.

The whisper cut through the chaos—steady, cold, absolute.

Left hand, now.

Emric pivoted low, his left hand catching her incoming strike and throwing her off balance. He thrust his palm upward. Arcane power roared through him, bursting out in a spiraling blast that hit Shaylee square in the chest.

Her body flared with light. For a heartbeat, she stood just above him, dissolving, eyes locked on his.

Then she smiled and winked. "I knew I chose right."

Emric's stomach flipped. His face went crimson. *Did—did she actually mean it?*

Then she was gone, ripped back to the respawn chamber in a burst of light.

Emric dropped to the ground, trembling, lungs burning, his health and mana bars scraping the bottom of his barrel.

He'd won. Barely.

Zeb whooped in his ear.

Emric swallowed, pressed his finger to his crest, and triggered recall. White light spiraled up around him, lifting him toward the Keystone.

But just before the light sealed him away, he saw them.

Collin and Chase.

The newly respawned Fireballers stormed into the lane, ready to turn the tide.

Too late. Their eyes locked on Emric.

Chase's gun warped from a handgun into a missile launcher. He aimed and fired.

Emric closed his eyes.

Before the magic missile could impact, the recall light swallowed him whole.

When he opened his eyes, he was back at the Keystone.

Chapter 15

The middle tower exploded first.

Collin's summoning circle split the ground, flames roaring out of the glyph as wings tore into the sky. A red wyvern unfurled in a storm of fire and smoke, its roar shaking the whole arena.

Chase stood beneath it, his gun twisting and expanding, humming with electric charge until it locked into a mana railgun nearly as long as he was tall. Sparks raced along the barrel as he braced it against his shoulder.

"Open wide," Chase muttered.

He fired.

The rail shot screamed through the air, a bolt of compressed mana punching clean through the tower's crystalline heart. The wyvern dove immediately after, flame pouring over the point of impact. The entire structure shuddered, cracked, and collapsed in a rain of molten shards.

At the same moment, the top lane crystal shattered.

Tyler and his clone laughed in unison, their voices doubled and impossible to tell apart. One illusion and one human—both hammering at the tower with relentless precision. The massive spectral mace smashed the tower's side to pieces while the two-handed battle axe sliced through the crystal like shears through tissue paper. By the end, the two

Essence-Crested mages had reduced the tower to glittering dust.

And then the bottom lane groaned.

Nick had abandoned human form entirely, his body blazing with molten fire. Flames spilled from his arms as he slammed both hands down, molten veins spreading like a spiderweb through the solid crystal. Behind him, another Tyler clone fired a storm of ghostlight arrows into the melting tower—each arrow sinking into the magma and exploding after a heartbeat. The core erupted, bursting apart in fire and ghostlight.

All three towers fell at the same time.

The arena trembled with the force of it, the sound echoing like thunder across the map.

Emric staggered as the shockwave rippled through the Keystone gates. He had won the fight with Shaylee, but they were losing the war.

"Okay, okay—don't panic," Zeb's voice tumbled through the link, high and jittery. "It's just tier-one defenses, nothing to worry about. Even if it is all three at once, it's still far from over."

"Zeb." Kennedy's voice cut sharp as glass. "Shut up."

She and Madi were already sprinting down mid together, their figures flickering on the map projection above the Keystone. Kennedy's sigils spiraled around her hands,

Madi's starlight aura trailing like a comet burning through the atmosphere.

Emric charged out of the gates alongside Tamlin and Pax, both of whom had just respawned, light still fading from their forms. Pax looked grim, jaw tight, stone plates sliding across his arms, but not yet fully formed.

"I'm so stupid—" Pax began.

"Don't," Kennedy snapped over the channel. "We'll discuss it later. Just don't do it again."

Tamlin adjusted his cracked glasses, voice brisk but eager. "They'll be taking camps right now. That's what I'd do."

"Camps?" Pax frowned. "What are those?"

Zeb cut in quickly. "Normally they give gold or levels, but since this isn't a video game, the rulebook changes it. They get mercs and stronger lane minions, which means more pressure everywhere."

"Oh crap," Pax muttered.

Tamlin slowed as they reached the mid-lane fork. "I'll reinforce Madi and Kennedy. We need momentum back in mid after that fiasco."

"Sounds good," Emric said. "Pax, let's go bottom."

Pax nodded, though his eyes didn't leave the ground.

Their boots pounded over the moss as they caught up with their own minion wave—already being forced back. Pax slowed, eyes narrowing. "Uh… Emric?"

Emric saw it too.

Armored mercenaries, eyes glowing deep crimson, were pushing through the lane. Heavy shields, spiked flails—towering over the minions around them, each at least three times the size of a standard soldier.

"Are those…?" Pax's voice trailed off.

Emric spoke into the channel, his voice tight. "Confirmed. They took camps. Mercenaries are marching bottom, chewing through everything in their path."

Zeb hissed through the link. "I'm already seeing red dots stacking up across the whole map."

Kennedy groaned. "Great. So now we're fighting them *and* an army."

Emric didn't waste words. Complaining wouldn't help. He raised both palms and hurled a volley of Arcane Blasts into the first rank. The spells detonated, staggering one merc, but the others lifted their shields, barely breaking stride.

Pax gritted his teeth, stone grinding across his skin as his body hardened. "All right. Fine." He threw himself forward, covering himself in rock before leaping straight into the fray.

Pax smashed through the last of the mercenaries with a stone-plated fist, shards of armor scattering across the lane.

Emric followed with another volley of Arcane Blasts, burning down the stragglers.

The fight hadn't been difficult, but it had been necessary. Mercenaries carried buffs too strong for normal minions to counter, and towers didn't even register them as targets. If Vector hadn't stopped them, the wave would have rolled straight through their defenses.

But it had cost them time. Too much time.

"Bottom lane is clear," Emric reported, chest heaving.

"Same here," Madi's voice came through from mid.

Zeb's voice cut across the link, high and tense. "And while you guys were clearing lanes—guess where the Fireballers went?"

Emric pulled up his mana tag interface. His stomach dropped.

Five red dots. All pushing top.

Before he could tap his crest to recall, the ground shuddered, a low rumble rolling through the map.

Zeb's voice broke. "No, no, no! Top tier two just collapsed! They've got a direct line to our Keystone!"

Emric's pulse spiked. His mind raced for a plan.

"Everyone back," Tamlin barked. "Recall now. If we lose Keystone, it's over."

Five beams of white light flared across the lanes as Vector's players tapped their crests in unison. The world bent, pulling them back until the inner circle of the Keystone snapped into view.

They sprinted top, aiming to cut off the Fireballers before they reached the core.

Collin's wyvern—Emric recognized it now, a Rathalos from *Monster Hunter*—swooped low, fire raining down like the sky itself was breaking. Nick, still in fire-elemental form, slammed molten fists into the ground, sending a shockwave of flame rippling toward them.

Fire above. Fire below. No way to dodge both.

Before Emric could move, Tamlin's arm snapped forward. A small glass bottle arced through the air, white-blue liquid churning inside.

The vial struck the flames and detonated with a force far too great for its size, like a hurricane stuffed into a bottle.

A concussive shockwave ripped through the lane, hurling both teams back several yards. The Rathalos screeched and wheeled upward, blasted off its dive.

When the smoke cleared, Emric blinked in disbelief. The firestorm was gone—locked in place. The shockwave had flash-frozen it all: streams of flame suspended midair like a forest of burning icicles, the molten wave on the ground frozen into jagged glass. The flames crackled faintly, as if the world itself were holding its breath.

For a heartbeat, the battlefield was silent.

Everything—fire, ice, motion—was locked in suspension. For an instant, it didn't look real.

Emric's pulse thundered in his ears. His body screamed to move, but there was nowhere to go. Even the Rathalos flapped uneasily above, its wings scattering frost with every beat.

No one moved. No one breathed.

Then—

Tamlin, almost casually, reached into his belt pouch and flicked another vial underhand, like tossing a pebble into a fountain.

It hit the ground with a soft *tink* and shattered.

The reaction was tiny compared to the first vial—just a puff of white smoke and a hiss—but the effect rippled outward, invisible at first. The ice began to dissolve.

The suspended flames fractured like glass, breaking into a million shards of red-orange dust. The frozen shockwave on the ground cracked, lines spiderwebbing outward until all of it—every last frozen ember locked in stasis—dissolved like sand slipping through an hourglass.

In seconds, the battlefield was bare stone and moss again. No fire, no ice, just two teams staring each other down.

The silence stretched.

Emric's chest heaved, every muscle wound tight. Across the lane, Collin idly shuffled his summoning cards while the Rathalos circled high above. Chase's railgun hummed with building charge. Nick burned like a living bonfire. Tyler and his clone shifted their weapons in eerie sync, spectral steel catching the light.

Shaylee wasn't visible, but Emric would have been surprised if she was.

He flexed his fingers, mana sparking across his knuckles. Through the mana-tag link, he caught Kennedy's steady breathing, Pax's low growl, and—of all things—Madi quietly humming *High Hopes* by Panic! at the Disco.

The absurdity of it broke through his fear, pulling a quick grin across his face.

The Rathalos' cry ripped the silence apart, and in the same heartbeat, the battlefield erupted into motion.

Emric raised both hands and unleashed a volley of Arcane Blasts.

Nick fired back with a barrage of firebolts. The spells collided midair, bursting into a blinding spray of sparks.

Above, the Rathalos dove with wings tucked and talons outstretched like blades. Fire swirled in its throat, burning like a miniature sun.

Kennedy ducked, but she wasn't going to make it.

The ground shook as Pax surged forward, stone layering thick across his frame. He grew—swelled—until he towered above the lane's trees, his full golem form unleashed. He planted one foot and leapt.

The Rathalos roared, flames spilling from its jaws, only for Pax's massive arms to close around its neck and wings, halting its descent.

For a heartbeat, stone and dragon wrestled above the battlefield. Wings beat furiously, claws shrieked against Pax's rocky armor. Pax bellowed with strain, veins of green mana blazing bright across his body.

Then he heaved.

The Rathalos crashed downward like a meteor.

Collin's eyes widened a split second before impact, and then the wyvern slammed him flat, light bursting as Collin was erased beneath his own summon.

Pax landed in a crouch, rubble scattering, stone shoulders grinding back into place. He looked over at Kennedy, managed a grin, and said, "Not on my watch."

She smiled back, eyes bright.

Then a rune flared.

Scarlet sigils bloomed beneath Pax's form, twisting tendrils of crimson light rising like a kraken from the deep. The glow climbed his entire body in an instant.

Pax's eyes widened. "What—?"

The sound died in his throat. A heartbeat later, the crimson light vanished, along with his stone armor. His massive frame collapsed, plates of rock falling away until only Pax remained—thin, human, vulnerable.

Shaylee flickered into view beside him, her veil peeling back like a curtain. For a heartbeat, she was visible to them all. Emric's gaze caught on her glacial blue eyes and the way her dirty-blonde hair looked flawless, untouched by battle.

He hated that he noticed.

She leaned close—close enough to whisper in Pax's ear. "Checkmate."

Her shadow dagger slid across his chest. Darkness burst outward like a tide, and Pax vanished in a flash of light, ripped back to respawn.

Before she slipped back into the veil, Shaylee lifted her gaze to Emric. She smiled. Winked.

Emric's stomach lurched. Fury twisted inside him, but heat betrayed him, flooding his face despite everything.

Off to the side, Madi's breath caught. She flushed red, eyes darting between Shaylee and Emric.

And then Shaylee was gone, swallowed back into the shadows as if she'd never been there at all.

The battlefield snapped back into motion the instant she vanished.

Nick surged forward, molten fire spilling from his arms, each step leaving smoking craters in the moss. He thrust both hands out, and a torrent of flame erupted like a living inferno.

“MOVE!” Tamlin barked. He lunged, grabbing Kennedy by the arm and dragging her backward.

She didn’t resist. Her eyes were locked on the space where Pax had fallen, her chest tight with guilt. He’d gone down right in front of her—because of her.

If she’d been quicker, stronger, he wouldn’t have needed to throw himself in front of her at all.

The wall of fire scorched the lane a heartbeat later, searing the space where she’d stood moments before.

Above them, thunder cracked.

Chase’s railgun hummed to life, white-hot, sparks dancing along its barrel. He braced, lined up the shot straight at Madi—and grinned.

But Madi wasn’t paying attention.

Her eyes were distant, unfocused, her lips moving faintly as if caught in a thought no one else could hear.

Light swallowed her as the blast caught her square in the chest. She vanished in a flash—KO’d. The bolt didn’t stop. It punched straight through into the Keystone.

A dull explosion shook the ground, dust and fragments spilling from the Keystone's crystalline heart.

"No!" Emric's voice cracked as the shockwave rattled his teeth.

He forced himself upright, fists sparking with mana. If they didn't turn this around now, they were finished.

The Keystone shuddered again, cracks spiderwebbing across its glowing surface.

Chase swung his railgun around, eyes sharp, the barrel humming as the air shimmered from the charge.

He aimed at Emric.

For a heartbeat, Emric froze—like a deer in headlights. He remembered Madi's body dissolving in recall, light flashed in his mind, followed by the image of the Keystone cracking under the last shot.

Then came the whisper.

Remember.

"Remember?" he thought, panic clawing up his throat. "Remember what?"

His chest tightened. He wanted to run, to raise his Arcane Bulwark—but it was still cooling down. Over a minute left.

The railgun fired.

The bolt screamed toward him, a condensed spear of pure mana—

And then it came.

Unbidden.

Pushed into his mind with brutal clarity.

New York. The schoolyard. That one stray arcane bolt—meant only to scare the younger kids. How he hadn't planned, hadn't thought—how he'd just raised his hand, and the bolt had stopped.

He thrust out his hand.

The rail shot froze.

Inches from his palm, the crackling bolt hung suspended, snarling with unstable power.

The battlefield went still.

Emric's arm trembled, sweat pouring down his face. He didn't understand how, but it was working.

His fingers curled. The bolt screamed.

Then he turned his wrist.

The rail shot whipped back across the battlefield.

Chase's eyes widened. "What the—"

The bolt tore past him and slammed into Tyler—the real one.

For a split second, the essence mage's eyes went wide with shock. Then he, and every clone linked to him, burst into light.

Gone.

The silence that followed was deafening.

Emric stared at his hands, unable to process what he'd just done.

"Emric!" Tamlin's voice broke through the chaos, half awe, half terror. "You—how did you—"

He never finished.

A ripple of shadow bloomed behind Tamlin.

Before he could turn, a dagger slid clean through his ribs.

His body dissolved into light before his question ever reached the air.

Kennedy spun, hands glowing with nature mana. "No!" She hurled a storm of what looked like glowing bubbles—fast enough to shred stone.

The shadows slipped past them like water.

Shaylee appeared behind her, one hand resting almost tenderly over Kennedy's shoulder. Then came the strike—one clean line of shadow through her core.

Kennedy's scream cut short as her body dissolved into recall light.

“KENNEDY!” Emric shouted.

And then Shaylee was there.

Right in front of him.

No veil. No shadow.

Just her.

She leaned close, her breath warm against his skin. For a heartbeat, time slowed.

Her lips brushed his in the faintest kiss.

Emric hesitated—fury colliding with a heat that betrayed him. He hated that he liked it so much.

Her smile curved, calm and certain. “See you around,” she whispered.

The dagger slid into his chest.

His world shattered into light, her smirk and wink the last thing etched into his vision.

Behind him, the Keystone pulsed once.

Twice.

Then exploded in a burst of flame and crystal.

The Fireballers had won.

Chapter 16

The recall light faded. Emric dropped to one knee.

His hand braced against the cold stone of the Keystone platform, lungs heaving like he'd run a marathon through fire. His heart wouldn't slow. He didn't know if it was the loss, the kiss, or the fact that he hadn't even tried to dodge at the end.

There were no cheering crowds, no closing announcements. No dramatic slow-mo outro. Just that awful silence—the kind that happened right after an earthquake's last rumble, when every creak and breath felt too sharp, too close.

Madi was suddenly next to him in a swirl of white light. She stood still for a second, face unreadable, hair falling across one eye.

He noticed Tamlin, Pax, and Kennedy as well.

No one said a word.

They didn't have to. Their walkout of the arena said it all.

Kennedy's expression was stone. Tamlin's head was down, glasses cracked. Pax walked like he wasn't sure he deserved to. Madi kept sneaking glances at Emric but looked away the moment he noticed.

They passed through the central tunnel, shoes echoing on stone, shadows stretching long from the arena lights behind them. Up ahead, the player gate opened to let them exit toward Highvel Hall. Just before they crossed the threshold—

“Hey!” a voice called behind them.

Emric turned, expecting a jeer, maybe a taunt from Chase or Collin.

Instead, Nick jogged up the corridor, still glowing faintly from the last of his fireform. His eyes were steady, tired—but not unkind.

Emric relaxed a bit. “Oh, hey, Nick.”

Nick came to a stop just in front of him. “You’re a right pain,” he said, deadpan. Then he smirked. “But cheers for that.”

“...What?”

Nick shrugged. “For keeping it clean. You could’ve gone for a dirty finisher. Didn’t. And—” he continued kindly, “we didn’t think anybody would ever get Shaylee or Collin’s Rathalos, but you got both of them.” He nodded at Pax. “That’s not nothing. You were much more than we expected.”

Nick offered Emric a hand.

Emric stared, then shook it.

“Thanks,” he said. “Right back at you. You guys were incredible.”

"Don't worry about it too much," Nick added with another smirk. "It was just a scrim—and if you ever don't get back up, that's when you really lose."

Emric smiled. "You'd better bring that kind of fire in the real tournament."

Nick turned and jogged back toward the rest of his team.

Emric turned to face his own—

But they were gone.

And Kael was waiting.

He stood in the center of the corridor, just past the gate's arch. His black cloak billowed faintly with mana static. Arms crossed. Eyes burning.

He stared at Emric as if daring him to come closer.

Emric's pulse jumped. His teammates were still just ahead—he saw them glancing back at him, giving Kael a very wide berth as they passed. No one said a word.

Kael didn't move. Didn't even acknowledge them.

He only had eyes for his little brother.

Emric approached cautiously, not sure what this was about—but already dreading the answer.

When Emric got about ten feet from him, Kael finally spoke.

"You hesitated," Kael said, low and sharp. "And because you hesitated, they lost."

Emric felt the air thicken, like gravity had just quadrupled. He opened his mouth—then closed it again.

Kael turned on his heel and started walking.

"Come on," he said.

It wasn't a request.

Kael's cloak swayed as he strode through the corridor, moving fast, clearly frustrated with Emric's performance in the match. Emric trailed behind, the echo of his shoes too loud in the suffocating silence. He hadn't realized Kael would be watching.

Kael didn't look back as he spoke.

"Why?!" he said, each word low and sharp. "Why did I spend all those nights beating hesitation out of you—just for you to choke the moment it actually mattered?"

Emric's stomach lurched. He knew that was coming.

The words hit him like a slap. He glanced back down the hall, but his teammates were already gone. Shadows swallowed the light of the archway.

Kael's boots never slowed.

A few weeks ago.

"That's a normal thing to do," Emric said, trying not to sound like it was one of the biggest achievements of his life.

Nia slapped the table, delighted. "She sounds perfect for you. She's kind and funny and likes the quiet—just like you. Brother, these are all green flags."

"It's not—I mean, it's just—we're building a team!"

"Uh-huh," Nia said, practically vibrating out of her chair. "I cannot wait to tell Katie," she said as she ran out of the kitchen and into her room.

Emric sat there a moment, blank. Then he picked up his backpack and headed to his room.

But before he could reach his door, a shadow filled the hall. Kael stood there, arms crossed, expression carved from stone.

"You just got your crest," Kael said, glaring. "And you're already in a tournament? You need help if you don't want to drag our family name through the mud. Come with me."

Emric hesitated. "I, uh—"

"Now."

There was no room for choice.

They ended up outside Kael's workshop, where he went every day for work. The night air carried the hum of wards from neighboring towers, the city glowing beneath them in veins of blue and gold.

"First rule," Kael said, creating a giant glowing sledgehammer out of mana, "you don't think. Thinking leads to hesitation. Hesitation leads to losing, or worse." Kael glared, eyes narrowing.

Emric looked away, guilty.

Kael continued, "Get ready."

Emric looked shocked. "But—spells take concentration, don't they? You have to think—"

"No!" Kael yelled, swinging his massive sledgehammer straight for the top of Emric's head. "Casting takes instinct. You hesitate, even for half a breath, you lose."

Emric jumped out of the way just in time. The hammer crushed the concrete where he had just been standing. Kael wasn't playing around. If he'd been a second slower, that hammer would have crushed his head like a tomato.

Kael stepped closer, voice dripping with anger. "You hesitated—" Kael swung again.

Emric dodged, barely.

"—and that's why our mother is dead."

Emric flinched. Not at the swing, but at the words.

His stomach hollowed. He'd been nine. Just nine. He remembered the black and green fire of necromantic magic. The way she shoved him back, shouting for him to run. His body had locked up. He hadn't moved until it was too late.

His hands trembled now just as they had then. "I—I didn't—"

“You hesitated. And she died protecting you.” Kael’s voice never cracked. It was iron. “So, you don’t get to freeze again. Not ever.”

He took another swing at Emric with the massive sledgehammer.

The guilt tore through him all over again, sharper than glass.

No more hesitating.

Emric thrust his hands out—right before the sledgehammer crushed his skull. An Arcane Explosion erupted from him, sending Kael’s mana construct flying.

Kael walked closer. “From now on, I’m training you. You’ll cast until it’s a reflex. No hesitation. No thought. Just act.”

And he did.

Hours passed that night. Kael was relentless; he kept coming and coming at Emric. First was the sledgehammer, then hands wrapped in what looked like glowing boxing gloves with massive spikes. “You won’t always see the weapon. What then?” Then, a glowing magical chainsaw, “Fear doesn’t wait for you to think.” Finally, he used an actual mana-constructed gun. “Hesitate here, and you’re dead before you even know it.” The gun’s barrel glowed bright blue, aimed squarely between Emric’s eyes. The hum drilled into his skull.

It felt like Kael was trying to kill him.

The whole time, Emric didn't complain. He knew this was a long time coming. And he kept hearing Kael's words: *You don't get to hesitate again. Not ever.*

Back in the present.

They turned the last corner. The Vale apartment door loomed ahead.

Kael finally slowed, just enough to glance back at Emric. His eyes were sharp, merciless.

"You hesitated today," he said again. "And because you did, your whole team paid the price. Do you understand me?"

Emric's chest felt crushed in a vise. He opened his mouth to speak, but the words caught in his throat.

Kael didn't wait for an answer. He pushed the apartment door open and strode inside, his voice trailing behind him like a command Emric would never shake.

"Hesitation kills."

Emric's lungs burned, his hands trembling. But in the back of his mind, the words pounded like a drumbeat.

Don't hesitate. Not ever again...

Chapter 17

Emric stood in the entryway, the air so thick he could almost see it. Kael hung his cloak on the rack with deliberate precision and didn't say another word.

Emric felt the silence press on his ribs harder than Kael's hammer ever had. He wanted to speak—to defend himself, to explain, to shout that it hadn't been hesitation that stopped him—but who was he trying to fool? That was a lie, and he knew it.

Kael disappeared down the hall without looking back. His door clicked shut.

Emric was alone.

He leaned against the wall, pulse still hammering, his body thrumming with exhaustion that wasn't just physical. His palms itched with leftover mana. He flexed his fingers, then curled them tight into fists.

Don't hesitate. Not ever again.

The words didn't sound like his anymore. They sounded like Kael's.

He pushed off the wall and slowly walked toward his room. His backpack was still slung over one shoulder, heavy with books and half-scribbled notes about coordination and strategy. A lot of good those had done for him.

When he passed Nia's door, he heard faint laughter from within, muffled by music. For half a second, he thought about knocking. But what would he even say?

His hand hovered near her doorframe, ready to knock. Then it dropped.

He closed himself in his room, sank onto his bed, and pressed his palms to his eyes. Every breath rattled. His chest wouldn't unclench.

He'd lost.

His team had lost.

He'd hesitated *again.*

Kael had seen it.

This wasn't about a scrimmage match anymore.

And worst of all, he wasn't sure Kael was wrong.

The aetherplate hummed to life on Emric's wall, a faint blue glow spilling across the clutter of books and notes.

He groaned. He didn't want to talk to anyone. Not Kael. Not Nia. Not the team. Not—

His hand moved on reflex, muscle memory kicking in before his brain could stop it. He answered the call.

The screen shimmered, and Miles's grin filled the display. He was chewing a big wad of his favorite purple gum, like always, popping a bubble before leaning close to his own aetherplate.

“Dude!” Miles crowed. “The new patch dropped today. You ready to get at it?”

Emric froze. He hadn’t even meant to answer. Fury flared hot in his chest—not at Miles, but at himself. He couldn’t even avoid talking to someone correctly; he’d managed to mess that up too.

“I was thinking with the new buffs I would try—” Miles’s smile faltered. He chewed more slowly; the rhythm was off, like a song slipping out of tune. “Whoa. You look like trash, man.”

Emric rubbed a hand down his face. “Thanks. I needed that pep talk.”

Miles leaned closer, squinting. “What happened? Wait... is this about the practice match you were hyped for?”

Emric stiffened.

Miles sighed through his nose, quiet but knowing. “You’re blaming yourself.”

They both knew they weren’t talking about the match anymore.

Emric’s jaw tightened. He looked away from the screen, not wanting Miles to see the tears forming in his eyes.

Miles's voice softened. "Emric... you've gotta stop doing that. You've been carrying that night with your mom for years, like it's the only page in your story. But it's not. That moment wasn't the whole of you. It never was."

"You think you're defined by that one moment. You're not. Life isn't one moment—it's billions. And they're happening all around us, all the time. What defines you isn't what you did back then, it's what you choose to do in the next moment. And the one after that. And the one after that. Every single breath is another chance to choose. Another chance to be different."

Miles leaned back, eyes closing, chewing his gum again—slow, steady, back in rhythm. "Your mom wouldn't have wanted you stuck in a prison you built yourself. I've known you forever, man. And right here, right now, is one of those moments. This moment could be your new starting line. You've got something in you. We all see it."

Emric swallowed hard, eyes red from the tears.

Miles sat up straighter. "Ask yourself this: what would your mom want you to do?"

For the first time since stepping off the field, Emric felt something shift in his chest. Not relief. Not forgiveness. But the faintest edge of possibility.

He exhaled, shaky. "You know... you're annoyingly good at real pep talks, man. You know that?"

Miles grinned, lopsided and warm. "Yeah, I get that a lot. Now—tell me you at least recorded the match so I can watch you lose."

Emric managed a laugh. Small, but genuine.

Miles relaxed even more. "That's better. Alright, man. I'll let you crash before you pass out on me. But tomorrow—we're running a new strat because of the patch."

Emric smiled.

Miles leaned forward and clicked the connection off.

The room went dark. Silence fell again.

For a moment, Emric just sat there in his room, the small smile still on his face. His chest felt lighter—but not free.

Kael's voice echoed like a shout across a cavern: *Hesitation kills.*

Miles's voice cut through just as sharp: *Life isn't one moment.*

The words overlapped until they weren't Kael's or Miles's anymore. They just lived inside him, fighting for space.

He leaned back onto his bed, staring at the ceiling. His body was drained, but his mind refused to quit.

He fell asleep without even realizing it. The next thing he knew, dawn light spilled across his room.

Chapter 18

The morning light slanted through Highveil Hall's vaulted windows, painting the corridor in bands of gold and pale blue. Students were scattered throughout the common area—some on beanbags, others on staircases or sprawled across the floor. The low thrum of chatter filled the space, but Emric barely registered any of it.

His shoes squeaked against the polished floor as he shuffled in. His bag hung heavy on one shoulder. His chest still felt tight, like Kael's words had carved themselves into his ribs overnight. He hadn't expected the silence in his head to feel heavier than the noise.

He braced himself for icy stares from his team. Maybe awkward silence. Maybe pity. Maybe Kennedy's trademark *I cannot even eye-roll.*

What he didn't brace for—what his brain outright rejected—was the sound of Madi's laughter.

His eyes darted across the hall.

At the far end of the room sat Madi and Shaylee, shoulder to shoulder on a floating bench near the window.

Laughing.

Like best friends.

Emric froze mid-step, nearly dropping his bag.

Shaylee leaned back, one boot hooked over the other, her cloak draped lazily behind her, effortless as ever. Her hair fell loose and perfect over her shoulders, not a trace of last night's duel left on her. She smirked at something Madi said and popped a grape into her mouth like she owned the whole room.

Madi looked more relaxed than Emric had ever seen her. Her starlight eyes were bright, her grin wide. She flicked her staff against the table as she told some story, and Shaylee snorted into her hand.

Emric blinked hard. Once. Twice. Nope—still real. Still happening.

He told his legs to move, but they refused. His body locked up in the entryway like the floor itself had cast a hold spell.

Madi and Shaylee. Together. Laughing.

He had prepared for a lot of things that morning. This wasn't one of them.

"Vale."

Her voice cut straight through the noise of the hall.

Shaylee's eyes had already found him—glacial and sharp under lashes that made the look even more piercing than he remembered. Her smirk curved wider, as if she'd caught him doing something embarrassing, like standing frozen mid-step with one foot suspended.

Emric's stomach dropped. His bag strap nearly slipped off his shoulder.

"You planning to stand there all day," Shaylee called across the room, "or are you waiting for someone to hit resume?"

Madi snorted so hard she nearly knocked her staff from leaning against the bench.

Emric's ears burned, going bright red. His legs finally remembered how to move, though not gracefully. Every step echoed like a small explosion.

By the time he reached them, Shaylee was leaning back with her chin propped in one hand, eyes glinting with amusement. Madi grinned like she'd just been handed front-row tickets to *The Maestro's* next concert.

"Morning," Emric managed, his voice cracking halfway through the word.

"Morning," Madi echoed, a little too innocently.

Shaylee tilted her head. "You look nervous. What's up?"

"Nervous? I'm not nervous," Emric blurted, voice too fast and too defensive.

Madi raised an eyebrow. "You're definitely nervous."

"Am not!"

Shaylee popped another grape into her mouth, rolling it around before biting down. "Relax. I don't always kiss the people I kill."

Madi slapped a hand over her mouth but couldn't stop laughing.

Emric's brain short-circuited. Again.

Shaylee's smirk widened. She plucked another grape and held it up, rolling it between her fingers like she was weighing some grand philosophical truth. "You know," she said, "I expected you to be more fun after last night. Instead, you're standing here like…"

She gestured up and down from his head to his feet.

Madi grinned wider, clearly enjoying every second.

Emric finally found his voice. "I am fun!" he blurted. "I just—"

Both girls leaned in, waiting expectantly.

Emric blinked at them. His brain felt like it was trying to run three different programs at once, and all of them were glitching. He pointed vaguely at the space between them. "Since when are you... you two?"

Madi tilted her head. "Since this morning."

"Seriously? That's... weird."

"Seriously." She nudged Shaylee with her shoulder. "We ran into each other walking into an IHOP this morning. Talked for a bit. Turns out she's actually hilarious when she's not—"

"Killing people?" Shaylee offered smoothly.

"Exactly." Madi grinned.

Emric's jaw worked uselessly. He wanted to say something about betrayal or confusion or sanity. Instead, what came out was, "Breakfast? With *her*?"

Shaylee leaned forward, eyes glittering with mischief. "Relax, Vale. You're the only one I'm interested in."

As if *that* had been the thing he was worried about.

Emric's brain went into meltdown. "Wait—what? That's not—I wasn't—why would you even—" The words tangled together and crashed out of his mouth like a pile of falling books. His hands flailed helplessly, as if he could swat the conversation into a less humiliating direction.

Madi burst out laughing again, this time not even trying to hide it. Shaylee tilted her head and narrowed her eyes, watching him unravel with open delight—like a cat watching a mouse squirm.

"I don't—okay, listen," Emric tried again, stabbing a finger in Shaylee's direction. "Whatever *that* was supposed to mean, I wasn't—"

"Jealous?" Shaylee purred, cutting him off.

Emric's ears went an even deeper shade of scarlet. "I wasn't jealous!"

"You sound jealous," Madi teased, her grin wicked.

“Tell me, Vale,” Shaylee said, smirking, “were you more jealous that I went to breakfast with Madi, or that Madi went to breakfast with me?”

Emric’s eyes went wide—then the universe saved him.

“Hey, guys.”

Kennedy’s voice cut through the laughter. Emric spun to see her walking up—with Pax beside her. Their hands were intertwined, casual as anything, like it was no big deal.

Madi blinked. “Wait. What?”

Kennedy’s cheeks flushed a faint pink, but her chin lifted with her usual defiance. “Yeah. We’re dating. Got a problem with it?”

Madi shook her head, grinning widely.

Then Emric blurted, “NO. Nope. Zero problems. Not even one. This is—this is amazing. This is the best news I’ve heard all week!” He laughed a little too loudly, the relief practically radiating off him. “Honestly, perfect timing. So proud of you two. Love that for you.”

Madi smirked, clearly recognizing exactly what he was doing.

But Emric didn’t care. For the first time since stepping into the hall, the spotlight wasn’t on him anymore.

Zeb’s voice rang out from the stairs. “Hold up, what did I just walk into?”

He came bouncing down the stairs two steps at a time, coat flapping, grin plastered on his face. Tamlin followed behind, calm for once, hands in his pockets, glasses fresh off a mending spell, looking perfect.

Zeb skidded to a stop when he spotted Kennedy and Pax still holding hands. "Oh-ho-ho! I knew it. Didn't I say it? Called it. Pay up, Tamlin."

Tamlin sighed, though a faint smile tugged at his mouth. "You never called it. You just theorized it."

"That's basically the same thing," Zeb said, already digging through his bag like he was searching for an I told you so banner.

Kennedy groaned and rolled her eyes, but Pax only squeezed her hand tighter. That said more than any words could.

Madi leaned back, stifling a laugh. "Honestly, I think it's cute."

"Cute?" Shaylee echoed, smirking. "It's adorable. I love it.

Emric looked between them, voice jumping an octave. "Why are you all so happy? What's going on?"

"Why wouldn't we be?" Tamlin asked mildly. "They're together. We're still a team."

"But—we lost," Emric blurted. "You're not upset? Not even a little? Not at me? I cost us the match."

That made everyone pause. The laughter faded. Everyone went quiet. Emric's chest tightened under the sudden attention—until Zeb spoke.

"Bro," Zeb said, for once completely serious, "it was a practice match."

"Exactly," Tamlin added, calm and certain. "No stakes. No eliminations. We learn, we regroup, we get stronger. That's the point."

Madi nodded. "Losing just means we've got room to improve."

Pax grunted quietly, as if he already knew exactly what he needed to fix.

Kennedy gave his arm a squeeze. "And we already know we can rely on each other when it counts."

Emric's throat went dry. The words hit something deep. *Hesitation kills*—Kael's voice still echoed, cold and sharp. But his team wasn't acting like they'd failed. They weren't dragging the loss behind them like a corpse.

They'd left it in the arena, where it belonged.

He was the only one who hadn't.

And suddenly, it clicked. The weight on his chest had never been about the match. It was about *her*. That one night. That one hesitation that had burned itself into his bones.

He'd been punishing himself for it ever since—dragging his mother's death into every fight, every failure, every decision.

But this wasn't that night.

This wasn't life or death.

It was just a practice match.

And for the first time, he wondered what it might feel like to stop living as if every wrong move was the end of the world.

Tamlin adjusted his glasses, his voice returning to its usual enthusiasm. "As peer leader of our class," he said, "I officially declare the scrimmage a success."

Emric blinked. "A... success?"

Tamlin nodded. "We learned. We adapted. And we got to know more of our classmates. That's more important than a win or a loss."

Emric exhaled slowly. His chest still ached, but for the first time, it didn't feel like a burden he had to carry alone.

Chapter 19

A day before.

Tamlin kept his head down, the echo of their shoes sharp in the corridor. His glasses were cracked and spiderwebbed, but he didn't care. He could still see through them, even if the world looked fractured—like it was mocking him.

They passed Kael in silence. The man's black cloak crackled faintly with mana, his eyes locked on Emric like a predator waiting for the perfect moment to strike. The rest of the team gave him a wide berth, angling away without a word. Tamlin didn't blame them. Kael didn't even glance at the others. He only had eyes for his younger brother.

Tamlin lingered half a step back, watching as Emric approached his brother, tense and silent. He saw the weight settle on Emric's shoulders before Kael even spoke a word.

But Tamlin didn't stay to listen. He couldn't. His chest was already too tight, shame gnawing at his soul. The moment Shaylee's dagger slipped between his ribs kept replaying in his mind again and again, sharper than the blade itself. Kennedy's scream. The flash of recall light swallowing him whole while Shaylee vanished back into the veil.

His hands trembled. He shoved them into his pockets, walked faster, and didn't look back.

The Ethington estate loomed near the base of the Wasatch Mountains, carved almost seamlessly into the mountainside—pillars of marble, banners embroidered with the family crest, fountains warded to never stop running. None of it mattered. Tamlin barely saw the grandeur as he trudged through the front gate. He slipped inside, head low, praying he could reach his room unnoticed.

No such luck.

A servant waited just inside the hall, posture perfect, hands clasped neatly behind his back. Jed. Tamlin knew him well—Jed had practically raised him, steady and kind, where his father had only ever been exacting. One of a dozen attendants who rotated through the house, each trained to bow at the exact same angle, speak in the same careful tone.

"Dinner is prepared, young master Ethington," Jed said, dipping his head slightly. "Your father is expecting you."

Tamlin's throat locked. His father's books were still taught in lecture halls. His brother Owen was already being hailed as the next great Ethington prodigy. The family name glowed brighter with every generation—except his. He'd turned that brilliance into a disappointment.

"I'm not hungry," Tamlin muttered, clutching his satchel tighter against his side, as if the weight of his books might shield him from the truth.

Jed hesitated, concern softening his voice. "Are you feeling unwell, young master?"

“Yes, that’s it,” Tamlin said quickly, relief flooding over him for not having to invent an excuse. “I need to rest. Thank you, Jed.”

Jed bowed again, impassive as stone. “Very good, sir.” He turned and walked away, footsteps fading down the marble hall.

Tamlin stood there alone, fists clenched, heat crawling up his neck. Unwell. A lie. Another black mark on his family name. First a failure, now a liar. The truth, however, was much worse: he couldn’t stand to sit at that table tonight—not under the weight of those portraits. Generations of Ethington mages looking down on him, each one a master in their domain. His father. His grandfather. His great-grandfather. Every single one of them brilliant. Accomplished. Flawless.

And him? He’d been stabbed in a practice match. Then lied to Jed—Jed, who was more a friend than a servant.

It didn’t matter that it wasn’t an official match. It didn’t matter that it “didn’t count.” Every failure carried the weight of his entire family name. And if they’d seen him lose so disgracefully...

He’d been so proud when his father beamed at his appointment as peer leader. But now, that pride felt miles away.

Tamlin pressed a hand to his cracked glasses and shut his eyes. Shame burned hotter than any fire spell. Owen never faltered. Owen never hesitated. He'd always wanted to be just like his older brother.

He turned away from the dining hall and stepped back outside. He needed air. He needed space to think.

His shoes echoed against the cobblestones as he cut across campus, satchel bouncing against his side. He should have gone upstairs to his room. He should've buried himself in books—or worse—gone back to dinner and pretended everything was fine. Instead, his feet carried him where they always did when his thoughts got too loud: back toward campus.

It was unusually busy for a Sunday evening. The school allowed students to practice magic freely from seven to nine on weekends, and nearly every chamber was in use. Every chamber except one—the old practice room in the Bloom Wing, tucked between empty lecture halls. Of course, it would be that one. The same room where their team had first come together, bright-eyed and ready to take on the world.

Now, he unlocked the door almost without emotion.

The heavy wood swung open, revealing the vast practice hall within. Training dummies lined the walls, scarred from spellfire. Chalk runes crisscrossed the floor, faint glimmers of residual magic pulsing along their grooves. The air smelled faintly of ash and ozone—like the ghosts of every spell cast here still lingered.

Tamlin stepped inside and dropped his satchel. His fingers twitched toward his crest.

And the moment he closed his eyes, it hit him again.

The blade sliding past his guard. The sickening crack of his glasses on the floor as the recall light enveloped him. The world tilting as his body dissolved into light.

He staggered, breath hitching, one hand pressed against his ribs as if the dagger were still there.

Peer leader. Some leader.

What kind of leader made his team weaker? He'd shamed the Ethington name. He'd—

"Not again," Tamlin hissed. He forced his hand forward and fired a *Frost Bolt* at the nearest dummy, freezing it solid.

The blast hit with a sharp zip, like the sound of a zipper sealing suddenly. The room smelled fresh, like the first snowfall of the year.

He didn't stop. Spell after spell tore out of him—arcane missiles, walls of flame, shockwaves of pure force. He pushed until his arms trembled, until sweat soaked through his shirt, until his lungs screamed. But the memory wouldn't fade. He could still see it—his team falling one by one, his own body collapsing, shame ringing louder than the thunder of his spells.

At last, he slumped against the wall, sliding down until he hit the floor. His chest heaved. His cracked glasses fogged over from the heat of his rage.

I let them all down.

His voice came out hoarse, but it filled the chamber anyway. “I failed!”

A floorboard creaked.

Tamlin jolted upright, head snapping toward the door.

Someone came in.

A figure leaned just inside the frame, eyebrow raised, chewing on what looked like a Reese’s peanut butter cup.

Zeb.

Of course, it was Zeb—he was the student ward for the Bloom Wing, after all.

Tamlin hadn’t realized it was past nine already. He’d been furiously flinging spells for over three hours.

“Hey, Tamlin,” Zeb said around a mouthful of chocolate and peanut butter. He swallowed and wagged the wrapper. “Got a ward ping – Professor Jenkins set the wards to go off if anyone’s slinging spells after nine. Normally I’d, you know, report it...” He waved vaguely toward the hall. “But I figured I’d check first.”

Tamlin’s chest heaved, his shirt clinging with sweat. The phantom ache of the blade pulsed beneath his ribs.

"...How's it going?" Zeb asked, tone casual, like they'd just bumped into each other between classes.

Tamlin let out a sharp, humorless laugh. "How's it going? Fantastic. Brilliant. Just in here practicing how to get stabbed better next time."

Zeb didn't flinch. He just stepped all the way into the room and let the door swing shut behind him. The sound echoed.

"Cool," Zeb said lightly. "Mind if I watch?"

Tamlin's glare snapped toward him, hotter than an inferno. "This isn't a joke, Zeb. You think this is funny? You were all relying on me, and I failed you all. I'm the peer leader—I'm supposed to set an example. I failed you, I failed myself, and I failed my family, and you just stroll in here with candy in your mouth like it's Halloween!" His voice cracked on the last word, tangled with frustration and rage.

Zeb didn't answer right away. He just picked the other cup from the wrapper and began to eat that one as well. Then, with deliberate calm, he tossed the wrapper into the trash can and leaned against the wall.

"Yeah, you're right," Zeb said finally, voice calm—almost too calm. "Practice matches are a huge deal. Honestly, I don't know how we'll ever recover from this catastrophic blow to our reputations. I'm sure the entire school will be talking about it for years."

His eyes flicked toward Tamlin, steady and unreadable. "Or..." He shrugged one shoulder. "It was a scrim. Professor

Beck told us to run them. Nothing on the line. No records. No consequences. Just practice."

He tilted his head. "So why are you really in here, tearing yourself apart?"

Tamlin's throat tried to work, but no words came out. His chest hitched once, then again. He tried to swallow it back, but like a dam holding back too much water, the pressure broke, and suddenly his vision blurred. He pressed the heel of his palm against his shattered glasses, trying to block the heat stinging his eyes.

Zeb didn't say anything. He didn't move at first either. Then, quietly, he pushed off the wall, crossed the room, and sank down beside his friend.

Zeb didn't speak; he just let Tamlin cry. No judgment.

And maybe that was why, after a long silence, Tamlin finally whispered, voice raw and shaking, "I can't let them down."

The words hung in the air—heavy, final.

Zeb curled his legs up to his chest and hugged them, staring up at the ceiling wards, faintly pulsing overhead. For a long time, he didn't speak either. Then finally, his voice came quiet—low in a way Tamlin almost missed.

"You know," Zeb began, "my mom used to say I was born with gears instead of bones. I looked up to her more than anyone. She was the Fabrication Lab Liaison back in her day, and when I got the same role here at Cloudrest..." He let out a soft laugh without much humor. “I’d never seen her so proud. Like… proudest-mom-ever proud. I was on top of the world.”

Tamlin blinked through the blur in his eyes, turning his head just slightly toward him. Zeb wasn’t looking at him, though. His gaze stayed fixed on the ceiling, his voice steady but far away.

“And then I screwed it all up.” He shifted, resting his chin on his knees. “I was trying to make up with Nick—yeah, Fireballers’ captain Nick. Back in the day, we used to be best friends. Something stupid happened, so small I can’t even remember what it was now, but back then? It felt huge. It broke us. I missed him—still do, honestly. Only child, and he was the closest thing I had to a brother. So when I finally got access to the lab and its crystals, I thought I had the perfect way to fix it. I’d make him something—an apology gift.”

Zeb’s mouth twisted. “Except I miscalculated one variable. One. And instead of a neat little apology crystal... I accidentally built a bomb. Not the explodey kind, but the etiquette bomb, and suddenly the entire school hated me. I screwed up Nick’s chance with a girl he’d had a crush on for years. And on top of that, every single student in our academy was pissed at me. They still are.”

He dragged a hand down his face. “I humiliated him. And when I saw everyone staring, I thought, ‘That’s it. My life’s over.' Worse, I thought my mom would be ashamed of me—the one thing I swore I'd never let happen."

For the first time, Zeb's voice wavered, quiet and raw. "I'd never felt smaller. More useless. I thought I'd wrecked everything—my friendship with Nick, my work in the lab, and the one thing I had with my mom."

He finally dropped his gaze from the ceiling, looking at his hands. "And when my mom found out... do you know what she did?"

Tamlin shook his head faintly, hanging on every one of Zeb's words.

Zeb's mouth curled, half a smile, half disbelief. "She laughed. Hard. Said it was the funniest thing she'd ever heard. I was so shocked I couldn't even breathe. I thought I knew her. Thought I knew exactly what she expected from me—but all that pressure? That was me. My head. My expectations. Not hers."

His voice softened. "She hugged me and said it was the best kind of story—the kind you only get when things go sideways."

Zeb leaned back against the wall, eyes closing briefly. "That's when I realized something. Sometimes we pile so much weight onto ourselves that we can't breathe. We think we're dragging a whole family tree behind us. But most of the time, the only one crushing us... is us. And if you let it, that pressure will break you long before failure ever does."

Zeb finally turned his head, meeting Tamlin's eyes.

Tamlin didn't answer. He just sat there, shoulders slumped against the wall, Zeb's words pressing into him deeper than any reprimand his father could've given. For once, he didn't fight them. He just let the words sink in.

The two of them stayed that way, side by side, the only sound the faint hum of the wards overhead. No more spells. No more words. Just quiet.

Then Zeb shifted, breaking the silence. "Alright, philosopher hour's over. We should get out of here before the wards ping again and Professor Jenkins tears us a new one."

He stood, brushing off his pants, and offered Tamlin a hand. "C'mon. You wanna get some ice cream?"

Tamlin smiled faintly. For the first time all night, the weight on his chest felt just a little lighter. He reached up and took Zeb's hand.

Chapter 20

Kael stood like a statue of judgment in the hallway, the sharp scent of charged mana still lingering around him like smoke. The team passed him, giving him a wide berth.

Madi was looking at something a million miles away. Her shoes tapped too loudly on the tile. Her heart pounded louder.

Don't look at him. Don't look at him. Don't—

She looked.

Emric stood frozen, caught in the gaze of his older brother, face pale and stiff.

Why do you care? she thought, sharper than she meant to. You shouldn't care.

There was some... thing happening in her chest—a tight, messy, hot twist of feelings she didn't have a name for. Emric looked like he was unraveling—humiliated, furious, devastated—and for some stupid reason, that made her feel even worse.

And what made it worse? That kiss.

Shaylee's kiss.

It wasn't real. Obviously. It was a fake-out, right? A battlefield distraction. A classic misdirect to throw him off.

Still, she'd kissed him.

Right on the mouth. In front of *everyone*. And Emric hadn't jumped away.

Did he like it?

The image wouldn't leave her head—Shaylee, calm and composed; Emric, stunned and helpless. It played over and over like a broken record.

Why do I care?! Madi asked herself for the tenth time.

It was a clever duel tactic. Shaylee was just being... tactful. All show.

I'm not mad about the kiss. I'm mad that she thought it would work.

As if Emric would ever be into *her*.

Except... it *had* worked. That was the worst part. It made Emric freeze. She'd seen it from the respawn chamber—right there on the aetherplate.

A flicker of something in his eyes.

No, she told herself. *That's not why I'm mad.*

She stared at the floor as they exited the arena, heat rising in her face.

Kael and Emric faded behind her. The cold didn't.

Madi turned sharply before anyone could speak. "I'm heading home," she muttered, not waiting for replies.

The air outside hit her like a slap—brisk and bright, not enough to clear her head.

She walked faster.

The shuttle was half-empty, filled with the low drone of spellcasting advertisements and a soft instrumental track meant to calm commuters. It didn't help.

Madi slouched low in her seat, hugging her backpack, chin tucked into her hoodie, and tried to ignore the ache crawling up the back of her throat.

She was not going to cry.

Over a fake kiss.

From a girl she barely knew.

With a boy who was just on her team.

Nope. Absolutely not.

This isn't about him, she told herself. *It's about the loss. It's about how Shaylee was moving around the arena like she owned the place.*

That's what's bothering me.

That, the loss.

Her reflection in the window didn't look very convinced.

She turned away.

The shuttle lurched around a corner, city lights flickering through the enchanted glass. A set of arcane runes blinked overhead, announcing the next stop. Madi barely registered it.

She tried to redirect her thoughts—to think about the scrimmage in a purely tactical way. *Where had they gone wrong? What could she have done better? That's what practice is for, right? See where you can improve. Do better next time.*

How did Shaylee even manage to get close enough to Emric to kiss him?

But every patch of logic led back to the same stupid moment—Shaylee leaning in with that impossible smirk, Emric freezing, and *that stupid kiss.*

So what if he froze? she argued silently. *It was a dumb move. Dumb, reckless, manipulative, and—*

And why did it bother her so much?

She groaned and slumped deeper in the seat, yanking her hood farther over her head.

Her brain was trying to run three different simulations at once—angry, defensive, and confused—and none of them were working.

It wasn't even a real kiss.

But it looked real.

Even if it was—why did it matter? Emric wasn't hers. Not like that. He was her teammate. She'd never even thought about him like that.

She let out a slow breath, forcing her jaw to unclench.

The shuttle hissed to a stop.

Madi stood, shouldered her bag, and stepped into the cool evening air. Only her face registered the temperature change—her hoodie was still properly enchanted.

The walk from the shuttle station to her house was a short one, winding through a narrow neighborhood full of flickering porch lights and patchy lawns. She knew every crack in the pavement, every neighbor, every cat that crossed her path.

Usually, the walk helped her clear her head.

Tonight, it didn't.

By the time she reached her block, the only thing she'd managed to accomplish was inventing five fake reasons why she was upset:

—She was hungry.

—She was overtired.

—Emric's hesitation cost them the match. She was just being a good teammate and empathizing with him.

—Maybe she had a concussion.

—Maybe her allergies were acting up.

Her feet hit the steps leading up to her porch.

The light was on inside.

And so was the chaos.

The second Madi stepped through the door, a rubber ball ricocheted off the hallway wall and bounced past her head.

"STOP THROWING BALLS IN THE HOUSE!" her mom shouted from the kitchen, her voice already fraying at the edges.

A chorus of protests followed:

"He started it!"

"It was just one!"

"Mom, tell Jax to give back my mana tag!"

Madi barely had time to drop her bag before a toddler slammed into her legs with sticky hands and an unreasonably strong hug.

"MAAADIII," wailed Ruby, the youngest of the lot. "You're home! I thought you got lost!"

"Nope," Madi giggled, scooping up her little sister and planting a kiss on her cheek.

Their mom stood at the stove, trying to recover from the soup boiling over. Her ponytail was half undone, and her shirt bore fresh splotches of sweet potatoes—clearly Ruby's artistic input.

Madi stepped in like it was muscle memory.

"I've got Ruby," she said. "What else do you need?"

"Please, just make sure the soup doesn't boil over again," her mom said, already halfway into the next crisis. "Jax took Tori's mana tag, and they're about to fight. And I need to stop Milo and Emmy from playing ball in the house before they break something else."

Madi was already moving.

She sat Ruby in a chair. The little one grinned like Madi's return had solved the world. She stirred the pot, adjusted the heat.

From the other room, she could hear Jax insisting it was *his* mana tag and Tori just lost hers.

Madi's hand moved on instinct, catching the rubber ball mid-bounce before it hit the soup.

"Aww! Madi blocked it!" Milo groaned. Emmy giggled.

Madi shot them a side-eyed smirk. "Come eat," she called through the house.

Like a hive of bees responding to a scent, the swarm of siblings descended into the kitchen.

"Feet off the table," Madi said, pointing at Jax.

Jax grumbled but obeyed.

Her older sister, Elle, emerged from the basement with a laundry bin on her hip. “Thanks, Madi. I was gonna help Mom with dinner, but I got sidetracked folding clothes.”

“You’re good, Elle,” Madi said, smiling.

She moved through it all without a second thought.

She didn’t complain.

She didn’t snap.

She didn’t stop.

She just kept going—sorting, serving, fixing.

Helping her mom. Catching her siblings. Keeping the house from falling apart one moment at a time.

Eventually, the worst of it passed. Everyone was fed. Everyone was happy.

The dishes were mostly clean. Madi washed while Elle dried. The rest of the family watched Bluey on the aetherplate while Mom struggled to get Ruby into her nighttime diaper.

Madi hadn’t thought about the match in over an hour. She hadn’t thought about anything, really.

She was grateful there wasn’t any more room in her brain.

Eventually, the house wound down—bellies full, tantrums faded, laughter trailing into sleep—until only the quiet remained.

Madi moved through it in near silence, flicking off hallway lights, brushing her teeth, stepping over a half-built fort made from couch cushions and blankets.

Ruby was out cold in her little princess bed, one foot dangling off the side, her tiny arms choking her favorite teddy bear in a death grip. Jax was still up, messaging friends on his mana tag.

"Hey," Madi whispered.

Jax froze, caught like he'd been reaching into the cookie jar. He shut the tag off in a hurry and rolled over. The rest of their siblings were already asleep, packed into the room like sardines—three-tier bunks crammed into the small space.

Mom and Elle were both passed out on the couch, too worn out to make it to their beds.

The front door opened. Their dad stepped inside, shoulders slumped, smelling faintly of steel and smoke.

"Oh—hi, Madi," he said softly, smiling tiredly. "I didn't think anybody would still be up."

"Hi, Dad." She hugged him tight. "How was work?"

"Long," he admitted, pressing a kiss to the top of her head. "Started at five this morning. Had to beg the boss to let me leave before midnight. They were still swamped when I walked out."

She kissed his cheek. "Thank you for working so hard for us. I love you."

"I love you too, sweetie." He squeezed her back.

"I'm heading to bed. I'll see you in the morning?"

"Maybe," he said with a tired smile. "Depends what time they drag me back in."

Madi nodded and slipped into the room with her siblings. She didn't bother with the light. She climbed into the middle bunk of one of the triple stacks, the springs creaking under her weight.

The mattress dipped beneath her like it knew. Like it was just as tired as she was.

She didn't think.

She didn't cry.

She didn't relive the match.

There was no energy left to process anything.

Sleep claimed her fast, before she even realized it.

And for once, it was dreamless.

Chapter 21

The sound woke her before her alarm went off.

Heavy boots on the floorboards. The clink of keys. A tired sigh carried down the hallway.

Madi blinked into the dark, her body instinctively recognizing the rhythm. Dad was already up. Already moving. Already halfway out the door.

She looked at the clock. Five a.m. Seriously? She'd been hoping for at least another two hours of sleep. But she knew once she was awake, the chance of falling back asleep was practically zero.

Careful not to jostle the bunk frame, she slid out from the middle tier. Ruby stirred once on her little bed below, clutching her teddy tighter, then stilled. Madi held her breath, then padded toward the door, moving like a ghost through the sardine-packed room.

In the kitchen, her dad was lacing his boots. His work jacket was worn almost to tatters. A thermos sat next to a mug of coffee he'd clearly forgotten to drink.

"Oh—hey, kiddo," he said softly, smiling despite the bags under his eyes. "Didn't mean to wake you."

"You didn't," Madi lied, fiddling with the drawstring on her hoodie.

He stood, kissed her hair, then hefted his bag. “I'll see you tonight… maybe.”

“Be safe,” she whispered.

“Always.”

Before he disappeared out the door, he leaned down to kiss his wife softly on her head. She was still asleep next to their oldest daughter on the couch.

Even in sleep, a smile spread across her lips.

And then he was gone, the front door clicking shut behind him.

Madi lingered in the quiet kitchen, her bare feet cold against the tile. For a minute, she thought about crawling back into bed. But her stomach didn’t like that idea—it gave a loud growl. And the thought of lying there, staring at the underside of her brother’s bunk until sunrise, sounded worse than anything.

She sighed, padded back into her room, grabbed some fresh clothes, and dressed quickly in the bathroom. She snatched her bag from the chair and—without thinking—reached for her staff in the corner.

The polished wood was familiar, steady. After last night’s match, she wasn’t about to leave it behind.

Staff in hand, hoodie zipped, she slipped out the door.

The sky was still dark, just a thin line of blue brushing the mountaintops. She breathed in the cool air, wrapped her fingers tighter around her staff, and muttered to herself,

“Pancakes. I deserve pancakes.”

Her feet carried her toward her favorite restaurant: IHOP.

The entry ward pinged as Madi opened the door.

The scent of breakfast filled her nose—a heavy, syrupy mix of butter, eggs, waffles, and coffee. The kind of smell that clung to your clothes long after you left.

IHOP at six in the morning wasn’t like IHOP at normal hours. Half the lights were dimmed. The booths were mostly empty, save for one trucker-looking guy face-down in his pancakes and a pair of students at a table, probably doing a literal last-minute cram session before school.

A waitress in a blue apron shuffled past with the energy of someone who had already lived an entire day and still had five hours left on her shift.

It was... perfect.

Quiet.

The first real quiet since she’d left the arena last night.

Madi slipped into a booth by the window and leaned her staff against the seat beside her. She pulled her hoodie tighter, let herself sink into the vinyl cushion, and exhaled slowly.

No shouting, no Ruby needing a diaper change, no rubber balls flying past her head.

The waitress shuffled up, rune tablet ready. “What’ll it be, hon?”

“Uh—” Madi was caught off guard, still wallowing in the silence, and then suddenly aware of how long it had been since she’d eaten anything that wasn’t reheated leftovers. “Short stack. Scrambled eggs. And hot chocolate with pumpkin spice.”

The waitress gave a little grunt that might have been approval and her finger moved quickly over the rune tablet like it was skating on a sheet of ice. “Be out in a minute.”

Madi slumped back, pressing her forehead against the cool glass of the window. The street outside was in that magical in-between time: twilight. Not quite bright and not quite dark. She loved this time of day. The mountains glowed faintly, waiting for the sun to rise. Her reflection in the glass looked calm. That surprised her.

When the food came, steam rising off the pancakes, she dug in fast. Sweet and warm. Like a kiss—wait. A kiss? Her brain flickered with *the kiss...* again? The match, the ending—it all came rushing back.

And then the door ward pinged again.

Madi glanced up, already mid-bite of pancake.

She nearly choked. Seriously? Here? In her safe place?

Shaylee Rose.

But different.

Gone was the smirk of a cloaked predator. This Shaylee shuffled in with an exhausted look, hair half-tied in a messy knot. She carried herself less like an assassin and more like someone who'd lost a fight with her pillow.

She paused at the door, scanning the empty booths. Then her gaze landed on Madi—with her cheeks full of pancake. Trapped.

And Shaylee, to Madi's absolute shock, lit up.

She waved excitedly, like they were old friends bumping into each other at the mall—or, apparently, at an IHOP. "You're up too?!"

Before Madi could react, Shaylee strolled across the diner and slid into the booth opposite her, dropping into the vinyl with a dramatic sigh of relief.

Madi stared, eyes wide, mouth full.

"I'm so glad I ran into you," Shaylee said without missing a beat. "I had such a rough night."

Madi swallowed hard. Was this actually happening?

The waitress arrived with her rune tablet. Shaylee ordered like it was a standing breakfast date.

When the waitress left, Madi blurted, "Hi… why are you sitting with me?"

Shaylee arched a brow. “Wow. Cold. Most people say hello first.”

“I’m sorry,” Madi said quickly. “I didn’t get much sleep. My little sister was being a pill last night, and then my dad accidentally woke me up on his way to work.” She tried to make it sound casual, like she wasn’t totally horrified by what was going on.

Shaylee’s expression softened. “Yeah. My baby brother’s scream could wake the dead. Had the whole house up at four. He’s lucky he’s cute. Otherwise, I’d have already tried to sell him.” She gestured at her half-finished hair. “I bailed halfway through getting ready because if I stayed in that house one more second, I was going deaf. Waffles were the only answer.”

“You were up at four? I was up at five,” Madi admitted before she could stop herself. “And you have a baby brother? That’s… sweet. I’ve got a little sister who’s two, and she’s a handful.”

What was she doing? Stop talking!

Shaylee beamed. “Mine’s only two months old. Already plotting world domination, I can tell.”

Madi almost smiled. She stabbed her pancakes instead, trying to hold the line. “So, you’re… just here for breakfast?”

“Obviously. Why else would I come to IHOP at six in the morning?”

Against her better judgment, a smile tugged at her mouth anyway.

Shaylee leaned back as her waffles arrived, smothering the entire plate in raspberry syrup like she was trying to drown her food. "I love him, but more than once I've thought about sleeping in the bathtub just to get away from the crying. My mom's told me no multiple times, but I'm going to try it tonight. I'll be sneaky. What she doesn't know won't hurt her, right?"

Madi choked on a bite of pancake. She wasn't supposed to laugh. Not at Shaylee. But it slipped anyway, muffled behind her hand. "The bathtub? Seriously?"

"Desperate times," Shaylee said solemnly, then ruined it with a wide smile at her syrup-drenched plate.

Madi shook her head, stabbing at her eggs. "Okay, but at least your little brother is just loud. Ruby gets creative. Last week she tried to flush one of my enchanted bracelets down the toilet."

Shaylee's eyes went wide. "You're joking. Was it the same one you used on Collin and Chase last night?"

"The very same," Madi admitted, laughing.

"I am absolutely letting them know they got sent back to the Keystone by a toilet bracelet," Shaylee laughed—a real laugh, not the sly one from the battlefield, but a genuine, unguarded one. "Oh, they're gonna hate that."

“Okay, okay, I’ll trade you one,” Shaylee said, pointing her fork like it was a duel. “My little brother projectile-vomited during family dinner last week. Got my dad, the breadbasket, and the cat in one shot.”

Madi pressed her lips together, trying not to break. It didn’t work. She laughed—loud, startled, real. Both students cramming for school, turned their heads, but neither Shaylee nor Madi cared.

“That’s horribly awesome,” Madi said through her laughter.

For a moment, the silence between them was different. Not awkward. Not hostile. Just… quiet. The good kind. The kind that made the booth feel warmer, the food taste better.

Madi fiddled with her fork, the question gnawing at her until it slipped out before she could stop it.

“So... are you into Emric?”

Shaylee’s eyebrows shot up. She tilted her head, studying Madi with sharp, amused eyes. Then she smirked, but softer this time. “Yeah. I am. Why? You jealous?”

Heat slammed into Madi’s cheeks. “I—no—I mean—” She cut herself off, groaning into her hands. “Fine. Maybe. A little. Okay, yes. I like him too.” She finally admitted it—not just to Shaylee, but to herself.

Shaylee leaned back, nodding. “Well, it makes sense.”

Madi blinked. “That’s it?”

"What do you want me to say? That we're love-struck rivals now? That I'm gonna hiss at you across class or hex your locker?" Shaylee snorted, waving her fork like she was swatting away a fly. "That's dumb. I like him. You like him. Honestly, I'll bet half the school probably does. What's the big deal?"

Madi stared, caught off guard. "So, what, we're just... fine with this?"

Shaylee's grin widened, flashing just a bit of the sly confidence Madi remembered from the match. "Tell you what—let's make a pact. We don't hate each other over a boy. That's pathetic. If he ends up liking one of us, cool. If not? Also cool. But we don't waste a good breakfast on stupid drama. That's movie stuff. Not real life."

Madi hesitated. Her brain screamed at her to argue, to put distance back between them. But… she was right. That was stupid. That *was* something out of those ridiculous teen dramas, and it had never made sense to her anyway. Slowly, her mouth curved into a smile. She held out her pinky. "Deal."

Shaylee grinned, mouth full of waffle, and hooked her pinky with Madi's. The promise locked.

Madi glanced at the clock on the wall—and her stomach dropped. "Oh crap. We're gonna be late."

They both looked at their half-finished plates.

They shoveled down the rest of their breakfasts with zero dignity, slammed their fluxbags onto the payment plate, and sprinted out of the restaurant together.

Chapter 22

Emric stared at the glowing calendar rune above his desk. Somehow, three weeks had vanished since the scrimmage. Three weeks of Kael's brutal drills that left his arms trembling, of Beck's lectures that always sounded like he'd rather be napping, and of Team Vector slowly finding their rhythm again. In fact, their rhythm had never been stronger. Even stranger, they'd ended up on friendly terms with Nick and the rest of the Fireballers.

And now—the tournament begins tomorrow.

The thought stuck with him all morning, following him into Beck's class like a ghost.

Beck shuffled in right on the bell, hair sticking up like he'd just rolled out of bed. He dropped a stack of papers onto his desk with a thump, then leaned against it, pinching the bridge of his nose.

"I trust you all squandered your weekend," he said flatly. "That ends now. The Cloudrest Tournament begins tomorrow. Try not to humiliate me."

He flicked a finger in the air, and glowing runes bloomed above him, weaving into the shape of a bracket.

Madi sat up straighter, eyes scanning the board.

Round one. Team Vector vs. The Runebreakers.

Shaylee spotted it too. She grinned and bumped Madi's shoulder. "Guess you're going down early."

Madi grinned right back. "Not a chance."

On the other side of the bracket: The Fireballers. Emric let out a slow breath. They wouldn't face Nick's team unless both sides clawed their way to the finals.

"Consider yourselves lucky," Beck said, his tone so flat it was impossible to tell if he meant it. "The draw could've been worse. Or better. Or both. I'm not your therapist."

He waved his hand again, and the bracket vanished. "That's it. Class dismissed. Don't screw this up. Or do. I get paid either way."

The runes flickered out, leaving only murmurs and shifting chairs.

Madi turned in her seat, grinning at Shaylee. "We're gonna crush the Runebreakers!"

"I know," Shaylee laughed. "With the stuff you and I have been working on, they're not going to stand a chance. You guys are going to win; I just know it!"

Zeb leaned over from the next row, holding a half-eaten Snickers bar. "Runebreakers sound like a metal band. Maybe we should form a band too—get matching jackets."

Madi's ears perked up at "matching jackets."

"Zeb," Tamlin sighed, "we're not forming a band."

“Yet,” Zeb countered through a mouthful of chocolate and peanuts.

The Fireballers drifted over from the other side of the room. Nick offered Emric a fist bump, which he returned without hesitation.

“Looks like we’re on opposite ends of the bracket,” Nick said, his accent giving a lazy drawl. “Reckon we might only cross paths in the finals.”

“Yeah,” Emric said, a flicker of anticipation in his chest. “Guess so.”

Nick’s grin crooked. “Good. Means I’ll have time to soften you up when it counts.” Then he tipped his chin at Zeb. “Don’t hold back, mate.”

“Wouldn’t dream of it,” Zeb shot back with a grin.

“Right-o.” Nick clapped Emric on the shoulder. “See you lot out there.”

The bell chimed. Students spilled out of the lecture hall in a rush, the low thrum of tournament excitement filling the corridors. Team Vector and the Fireballers broke apart with quick nods and good lucks, each group heading their own way.

Emric waved goodbye to his team, slung his bag over his shoulder, and made for home—anxious to tell Kael and Nia that his team was in the first round of the tournament.

The apartment door clicked shut behind him. Kael was already in the living room, watching the news. Nia sat next to him on the sofa—she must have rushed home early.

"Ah," Nia said brightly, "perfect timing. I just told Kael."

Emric blinked. "Told Kael what?"

"That my team and I are in the first round of the tournament tomorrow." Her tone was coy, almost teasing.

"What—no, you're not, it's my team that—" His stomach dropped as it hit him. Nia was on the Runebreakers.

"You're kidding."

Emric's voice cracked halfway up the register. He stood frozen in the doorway, bag still slung over his shoulder, like someone had swapped the rules of reality on him.

Nia smiled sweetly from the sofa—currently upside down, her head where a normal person's feet would be. "Do I look like I'm kidding?"

"You—" Emric stammered, dropping his bag with a heavy thump. "You've been at all our team meetings. You literally helped us run drills in the Bloom Wing!"

Nia giggled, flipping over onto the floor and landing neatly on her knees, eyes sparkling. "I know. Wasn't it fun?"

"Fun?" Emric's voice jumped another octave. "You were spying on us?"

She tilted her head, eyes rolling up as if searching her brain for the right phrasing. "Not spying. More like… playing the long game. And hey—how was I supposed to know we'd end up in round one together? Lucky break."

Kael, unmoved on the other end of the couch, finally let out a quiet chuckle. Arms crossed, eyes fixed on the news, but Emric knew he wasn't laughing at the anchor.

"You knew?" Emric snapped, whirling on him.

"No, but it makes even more sense why she's in the advanced track and you're not," he said, not breaking eye contact with the screen. He said it with a smirk.

Emric groaned, dragging both hands down his face. "This is insane. I'm reporting this to Mrs. Atkinson. It has to be a rule violation."

Nia giggled again. "She was the one who gave me the idea. She's a sneaky devil if you can get past her stories."

"That figures," Emric muttered.

Kael chuckled again, low and amused.

Nia stood, slinging her bag over her shoulder like she'd just won something. "Don't stress too much. I'll tell my team to take it easy on you." She winked, then darted for her room.

Emric opened his mouth, then stopped. Nothing he could say would fix this.

Out of the corner of his eye, he noticed it—the hallway. His dad's door.

It was cracked, just barely. A thin sliver of light glowed across the floor. Was he listening?

Emric sank onto the couch beside Kael with a groan.

Kael had switched the channel. A giant mech slugged a massive kaiju across the jaw, sparks flying. A minute later, the mech pulled a gleaming sword from its back.

Kael frowned. "Why wouldn't it just use the sword the whole time?"

Emric stared. "That's your takeaway right now?"

Kael smirked, eyes still on the screen. "What? It's a fair question."

Chapter 23

Emric awoke to the sound of a notification on his aetherplate. He reached up, aiming to slap the dismiss button without opening his eyes. Instead, he answered the call.

"EMRIC!!!"

He sat bolt upright, smacking his head on the shelf above his bed.

"Ow—wait—what is happening?"

"IT'S GAME DAY, BABY!"

The voice boomed again—unmistakably Miles. Emric flailed for the aetherplate on his desk and ended up falling out of bed. Miles started laughing.

From the floor, face pressed to the rug, Emric groaned, "You know it's like five in the morning here, right?"

"I sure do," Miles laughed, blowing another purple bubble. "But it's seven here, so it doesn't bother me."

"You're insane," Emric muttered.

"No," Miles replied in a bad British accent, "I'm supportive, my good chap."

Emric dragged himself up far enough to rest his chin on the desk in front of the screen.

He just laughed. “Thanks, man. I need to get ready and hop in the shower before I go.”

Miles smiled. “Yeah, I know. I just wanted to wish you good luck before I had to go to school.”

“Well, thanks for the wake-up call.” Emric grinned.

“Any time.” Miles flicked the call off.

Jed opened the door without knocking, as usual.

Ever since Tamlin was a boy, Jed hadn’t bothered with formality. Even though he served the family, he always seemed at home here.

Before even stepping inside, he began his rehearsed script. “Young master Tamlin, it is time to get out of—”

“No need this morning, Jed,” Tamlin interrupted.

“Up so early, sir?”

“Of course. Today is the big day.” Tamlin grinned with enthusiasm far too bright and chipper for this early hour.

Jed stepped in fully, tray balanced in his hands. “In that case, I presume this is good news. Your breakfast is ready in the dining area. Your brother and father are also awake.”

Tamlin gave a small nod. “Thanks, Jed.”

Jed lingered a moment, his voice softening. “You’ll do well. I know it.” Then he slipped out.

Tamlin lifted his chin, a spark of pride catching in his eyes. Today, he would not falter.

Kennedy tugged her bag higher on her shoulder as she stepped out the front door.

"Bye! I'll see you tonight—I hope you come to watch my match!" she called as she reached for the door to close it. No answer came from inside.

She shut the door firmly, taking a steadying breath before turning toward the street.

And froze.

Pax stood there, grinning, a dozen roses clutched awkwardly in his hands.

"Morning," he said, suddenly unsure if the flowers were romantic or just ridiculous.

Kennedy's face broke into a wide smile before she could stop herself. She wanted to play it cool, but she was too happy. She reached out, took the roses from him, and kissed him quickly on the lips.

"They're perfect," she said softly.

Pax beamed, relieved. "Good—because I bought chocolates too, but… uh… I ate them on the way here."

Kennedy lifted the flowers with a teasing smirk. "You're lucky I like roses better anyway."

He offered his arm. She took it without hesitation, and together they headed off toward the academy.

The IHOP door banged open, and Madi burst out first, staff clutched in one hand, her hoodie bouncing with every step. Shaylee followed close behind, still chewing the last bite of waffle, raspberry syrup faintly smeared at the corner of her mouth.

“Hold still,” Madi laughed, flicking her fingers in quick patterns. A starlight charm swirled through the air and settled neatly onto Shaylee’s hair, weaving the half-done braid into place. “Honestly, how do you leave the house like this?”

Shaylee grinned, tossing the finished braid back over her shoulder as they sprinted. “It’s called mystique.”

“Yeah, it’s called messy,” Madi shot back, but her grin gave her away.

They skidded around the corner toward the academy—

—and nearly ran into Zeb.

He was strolling down the street with all the urgency of a man headed to a nap, one hand tucked lazily behind his head, the other lifting a can of Mountain Dew. He tilted it back, chugged, and belched with satisfaction.

“Sup,” he said, not breaking stride.

Madi gaped. “That’s your pre-tournament breakfast?”

"You know it," Zeb replied smoothly. "Breakfast of champions."

Shaylee snorted. "More like breakfast of diabetes."

Zeb grinned sideways at her. "That's rich, coming from the girl with half a gallon of syrup still on her face."

Shaylee wiped at the corner of her mouth with the back of her hand, then smirked. "I was saving it for later."

The girls didn't slow down. Madi grabbed Zeb's free arm, Shaylee hooked the other, and before he could react, they had him half-dragged, half-running toward the academy.

"Wait—wait—my Dew!" he yelped, trying to keep the can upright as his feet scrambled to keep up.

It slipped from his grip anyway—plopping neatly into a recycle bin as they rushed past.

Zeb twisted back to watch it land. He muttered to himself, almost satisfied: "It's the little things."

And the three of them disappeared down the street together.

Emric got there first.

The academy gates loomed tall and bright in the morning sun, tournament banners fluttering in the wind. Workers were still chalking fresh wards into the flagstones, the runes glowing faintly blue as they activated. The whole campus felt awake but not yet alive—like a stage with the curtains down.

Emric shifted from foot to foot, bag slung over his shoulder. He checked his crest. Looked up. Checked it again. Fiddled with his strap. Adjusted his shoes. Back to his crest.

"You sure you checked your crest yet?"

Emric looked up. Tamlin was crossing the courtyard, uniform pressed, glasses gleaming like he'd been awake since dawn. He hadn't, of course—Miles had made sure Emric was the one awake at dawn. Tamlin had the composed walk of someone who belonged here—the exact opposite of Emric's jittering.

"You're early," Emric said.

"I'm always early." Tamlin planted his hands on his waist, chin high, the picture of peer-leader pride. "As peer leader, if I'm not ten minutes early, I'm five minutes late."

Emric just stared at him in his pose, at a loss for words.

"You look ridiculous standing like that," Kennedy's voice rang out.

She and Pax came up arm in arm, Kennedy clutching her bouquet of roses like it was a first-place trophy. Pax wore the goofy grin of someone convinced he was dating above his grade. He wasn't—but he thought he was. Emric smiled.

"Are those—"

"Roses from my boyfriend," Kennedy said, smug but glowing. "Jealous?"

Pax just smirked and shrugged. “She likes ’em.”

Kennedy squeezed his arm, her grin softening. “I love them.”

A smile settled over Emric’s face, and then—

“I was saving it for later!” a voice shouted from up the street. Everyone turned.

Madi was laughing as she and Shaylee sprinted closer, Shaylee’s braid finishing itself under a starlight charm. Zeb stumbled between them, dragged along by both arms, still clinging desperately to a Mountain Dew can.

“Wait—wait—my Dew!” he yelped.

The can slipped free and clattered neatly into a recycle bin as the trio passed.

Zeb twisted back to watch it land. He muttered something under his breath, too low for Emric to catch.

By the time they reached the gates, the whole team was there.

For a moment, nobody spoke.

The excitement crackled between them like a chain lightning spell, jumping from one to the next.

The arena bells tolled.

Low.

Heavy.

Final.

The sound rolled across the campus, shaking the banners, thrumming through the stone beneath their feet.

Emric glanced up at the looming arena, pulse racing.

Game day had begun.

Chapter 24

The locker room smelled faintly of cleaning potion, like someone had scrubbed it down extra just for today. Above them, the roar of the school crowd rumbled through the concrete ceiling, excitement thrumming like static in the air.

Emric sat at the end of the bench, lacing his shoes, checking his crest, glancing at his teammates. His nerves wouldn't let him sit still. His hands itched with magic. Any minute now, the wards would flare. The announcement would start.

Across from him, Tamlin was polishing his glasses for the third time in five minutes, muttering strategy like he was preparing for a deadly exam.

Zeb was sprawled back with his arms behind his head, calm as a sunbather.

"You guys stress way too much," he said, voice relaxed. "We've been training. We're solid. Plus, with the extra spells I slipped onto the mana tags, we'll have a leg up."

Tamlin blinked. "What kind of spells?"

"I linked them to the Pillar's database," Zeb replied smoothly. "We can scan more details on opposing teams now."

Tamlin sat straight up, scandalized. "Zeb! That doesn't sound even remotely ethical."

“All’s fair in love and war,” Zeb said with a shrug. “And this is definitely war.”

Before Tamlin could reply, Madi stepped over to Emric, hands clasped behind her back, cheeks glowing pink.

“I know you’re going to do great,” she said softly. “But I want you to have this. Just in case.”

She held out a ring. It gleamed with a deep violet hue, and inside the gem a flicker of flame twisted slowly, like it was alive.

“I made it myself,” she added. “It’s my first attempt at a new enchantment style I’ve been working on.”

Emric stared, stunned. A handmade enchantment — a personal one — this was huge. His chest tightened with warmth.

“Thank you,” he said sincerely. “It’s amazing. I… don’t have anything to give you, though.”

Madi laughed under her breath. “It’s not a trade, Emric. I wanted you to have it. No strings.”

Before he could say more, the locker room door creaked open.

Kael stood in the doorway, arms crossed, face unreadable — a statue carved from stone. His gaze locked onto Emric, and he gave a small nod: *come here.*

Madi blinked, visibly tensing. “Is he… gonna kill you?” she whispered.

“Let’s hope not,” Emric muttered, giving her an apologetic look. “One sec.”

“Uh huh…” she murmured, eyes glued to Kael.

Emric stepped into the hallway. The door swung shut behind him with a soft click.

Kael didn’t waste time.

“I’m not allowed in the locker room,” he said. “But you need to know a couple of things before this starts.”

“What’s up?”

Kael’s jaw tightened. “Dad’s here.”

Emric’s heart stopped. “What?”

“I told him,” Kael said, voice clipped. “Told him his daughter and son are in a tournament together. If he had any pride left as a father, he could get his lazy ass out of bed and show up.”

The words came with venom, tightly coiled.

Emric swallowed hard. His father hadn’t shown up for anything in years.

“...Did he actually come?”

Kael gave the smallest nod. “He’s in the crowd.”

Emric didn’t know how he felt about that — let alone what to say.

"There's one more thing," Kael said. His tone sharpened, steel slipping into it. "You're going up against Nia."

Emric blinked. "Yeah… I know."

"I need you to really *know* it," Kael said. "She's your sister, but this match isn't playtime. I didn't spend the last month drilling you just so you'd freeze when you see her out there."

"I won't."

"Good. Because Nia won't either."

Kael's eyes narrowed, hard and clear. "I'm serious, Emric. The truth is — I'm more confident in *her* ability than I am in yours. She knows what she's doing. She's smart. Tactical. She's not going to hesitate just because her older brother is standing on the other side of the map."

Something tightened in Emric's chest, not hurt exactly, just pressure.

"I'm not telling you to fight dirty," Kael said. "I'm telling you to fight like it matters."

Emric nodded once, steady. "It does matter to me, Kael."

A brief flicker of pride crossed Kael's face. He gave a short grunt of approval, then turned without another word and disappeared down the corridor.

Emric stood there a moment longer, letting the weight of it settle.

Nia. Their father. And Kael, believing in him…

Maybe he didn't hate him for their mother's death after all.

When Emric stepped back into the locker room, his heartbeat was still thudding from Kael's words. The buzz of voices and movement washed over him again, like someone had turned the volume back up.

Across the room, Madi and Shaylee were huddled together, whispering. As soon as they spotted him, both turned his way and immediately burst into giggles.

Madi tried to hide it behind her hand. Shaylee didn't even attempt it.

They gave him the same kind of sidelong look, the kind that made him wonder if he had something on his face, or worse, like they knew something he didn't.

He blinked, flustered. "What?"

Madi grinned and stepped toward him, Shaylee close behind. Heat crept up his cheeks.

Before they could reach him, the atmosphere shifted.

Kennedy sat curled on the far bench, knees pulled tight to her chest. Her face was hidden, but the tremble in her arms gave everything away.

Pax sat beside her with an arm around her back. He leaned close, forehead resting gently against hers as he spoke in a low, steady voice.

“They didn’t come,” Kennedy whispered, her voice cracking. “I waited, I kept looking, but they’re not here.”

Pax didn’t try to defend them. No excuses. No empty comfort.

He just held her tighter. “I’m here,” he said. “I’ll always be here.”

She looked up at him with shining eyes, then buried her face in his chest. Pax wrapped both arms around her like he could shield her from the whole world.

For a heartbeat, the locker room fell quiet.

The doors clanged open, snapping the moment clean in half.

Professor Beck strode in first, looking like he was already done with the entire event. Professor Moss followed, back to hooves, both hands and feet this time, and inexplicably, human ears. Tamlin snorted softly.

“Alright, team,” Beck said, his voice cutting across the room. “It’s time.”

Moss clapped his hooves together in what might have been applause. “Starting platforms are open. Time to show us what you can do.”

“Any last-minute spell tweaks or gear fixes,” Beck added, “handle them on the way to the gate. The window is closing.” He paused. “And unlike the scrimmage, merc camps will be under faculty control this time, so expect a fight. They will not go easy.”

His eyes swept over them. “Ready or not.”

Shaylee perked up. “Yay, good luck!” She hugged Madi and blew Emric a kiss.

His face went beet red.

Zeb stretched like he was waking from a nap. “Let’s get to it.”

Kennedy wiped her eyes, gave Pax’s hand a final squeeze, then stood and joined the others.

Emric rose with the team, squaring his shoulders. His pulse thundered louder than the roar of the stadium overhead.

Madi stepped beside him, close enough that their hands brush against each other.

Tamlin was already muttering formations under his breath, half to Emric and half to himself.

Together they filed out through the double doors, footsteps echoing down the corridor that led toward the starting platforms.

Ahead of them, the arena waited.

Above them, the whole school roared.

Emric slipped on Madi’s ring.

Chapter 25

His pulse thundered in Emric's ears as he stepped out of the tunnel and into the arena.

For a moment, he couldn't hear anything, just the drumbeat of his own heartbeat.

Which he knew was impossible, because the crowd was clearly going wild. Students were cheering, jumping, waving enchanted signs. But it all felt muffled, like sound couldn't reach him yet.

Banners for Team Vector and The Runebreakers rippled in opposite corners of the arena, crest magic glimmering along their edges.

He took a deep breath.

—and the volume snapped back in all at once.

Thunderous roars. Cheers. Magical noisemakers.

Runes flaring. Horns blaring. Streams of enchanted light streaking across the sky.

Morning sunlight poured through the glass ceiling above, refracting like a god's eye watching the field.

Team Vector stepped onto their crimson platform.

A dozen floating scry-cameras swooped in from every angle, casting each member's magnified image onto the massive skyboard overhead.

Emric's face appeared first, mid-blink.

He winced.

Tamlin came next, flashing a bright smile and two enormous thumbs-ups.

Madi grinned and waved enthusiastically toward Shaylee, who sat with Nick and the rest of the Fireballers in the upper stands, all cheering loudly.

Pax clapped Tamlin on the shoulder. "Don't worry. If you go down again, I'll avenge you with extreme overkill."

Kennedy rolled her eyes but smiled as she took his hand.

"Please don't say extreme overkill.' It's so dorky."

"I *am* dorky," Pax replied, waggling his eyebrows.

Kennedy laughed and kissed him on the cheek.

"Yeah, but you're *my* dork."

Zeb groaned. "We're so doomed."

"Focus," Tamlin snapped, but even his tone lacked its usual edge. There was a flutter of nerves under all that crisp control today.

Across the arena, the Runebreakers stepped out from their own tunnel.

They moved like a practiced strike team, robes woven with gleaming runic patterns, crest magic already glowing.

Nia led them.

Her expression was steady, but Emric caught it, a faint flicker of nerves.

She spotted him and gave a quick wave, cheeks already flushed.

He smiled and waved back.

To the east, the commentator box floated above the field.

Professor Beck's voice rolled across the arena, half-bored, half-annoyed as always.

"Welcome to this year's opening match: Team Vector versus The Runebreakers. Please direct your attention to the skyboard above the center of the arena."

A countdown appeared midair.

00:59

00:58

Professor Moss waved a hoof at the crowd, beaming.

"A reminder that there is no danger here today. With the wards active, no spell can breach the arena barrier. That means everyone in the stands is perfectly safe, and the combatants do not need to worry about collateral damage. So please, absolutely no holding back."

At the far end of the platform, Principal Grimm sat tall and silent. He wore no headset and added nothing.

The timer ticked to 00:30.

And just like during the scrimmage against the Fireballers—

the platforms beneath each team began to drift apart, gliding smoothly toward their respective Keystones.

Team Vector toward the glowing crimson spire.

The Runebreakers toward the cobalt one on the far side.

Madi drew one long breath, then another.

Emric locked eyes with Nia across the field.

The Keystone cores flared to life, flooding the arena in radiant light, one side red and the other blue.

With a familiar *shunk*, the platforms dropped the final few feet and locked neatly into cutouts in the stone floor. The impact triggered a ripple of crimson magic rolled across the arena's inner barrier.

The clock struck:

00:02

00:01

Begin.

Team Vector split at once.

Madi and Emric broke left, sprinting toward the top lane's moss-draped ridge, boots kicking up dust and old spell-ash as they ran.

Across the field, Pax and Kennedy vaulted the river crevice into mid-lane. Pax was already bulking into his golem form, earth crawling up his arms and shoulders in jagged plates. Kennedy flexed her fingers, and light surged between her palms, already gathering for the fight ahead.

Tamlin angled right, heading for the bottom lane, two potions already in hand. One shimmered midnight black; the other fizzed, colors shifting violently from green to orange and back again. His crest pulsed as he ran.

"Alright," Zeb's voice cracked through their tags, "no pressure or anything, but you're currently being watched by… oh, I don't know—the entire student body, faculty, a couple local news outlets, *and* probably YouTube."

"Helpful as always," Emric muttered with a smile.

Madi tightened her grip on her staff and shot him a sidelong look. "Think Nia's top?"

"I hope so," Emric said, breath already tight. "I'd rather face her sooner than later."

Madi grinned. "Careful. I hear she's vicious."

Emric smiled despite himself. "We'll be fine. When she was spying on us, I was watching her. I didn't realize it at the time, but I think I've got a plan."

They broke into a clearing. Ahead, Runebreaker silhouettes darted through the fog, players slipping into position.

Mid lane – Pax and Kennedy

The terrain narrowed into a natural corridor: broken cobblestone, tall hedgerows, and elemental trees rooted deep in the leylines. Pax's rocky frame grew with each step, stone fusing across his skin until he towered like a walking fortress.

"One just up ahead," he muttered.

Kennedy spread her arms, releasing a shimmering pulse of light that raced across the lane. The wave struck a hidden figure and lit him in a vibrant neon green. A Runebreaker, caught mid-channel.

"Got him," she called.

Pax slammed both fists into the ground, like two gigantic sledgehammers. Cracks spider-webbed down the lane, splitting the earth and forcing the channeler to leap aside. The spell broke.

The crowd roared.

"He'll probably call for backup now that we interrupted his channel. I'll bet it was a summoning spell." Kennedy said to Pax.

She tapped his shin. Green light surged up his body, reinforcing his armor with living stone.

Bottom Lane – Tamlin

Tamlin crouched behind the broken arc of a ruined tower relic, fingers tight around his potions. "Zeb, what am I looking at?"

“Emric and Madi have Nia and Lennox,” Zeb reported. “Pax and Kennedy are on Randy. Which means you’ve got Mike and Chris. Though one of them might rotate mid.”

“Wonderful,” Tamlin muttered. He lobbed the green-orange potion in a high arc.

It burst above the clashing minion waves, releasing a cascade of light. The Runebreaker minions shimmered—blue turning instantly crimson. Both sets of minions now marched together, a doubled swarm charging the enemy tower.

The Runebreakers scrambled to react, but both of them stayed. No mid-rotation.

Zeb’s tag feed flashed across Tamlin’s vision:

Chris Harper – Crest of Iron. Rank: B

Michael Quinn – Crest of Surge. Rank: A

Both had full bars on health, stamina, and mana, not surprisingly, the match just started. He then jumped out and immediately lobbed the midnight black potion at the pair before they noticed him. They were busy trying to clear the double-sized minion wave before it took the tower’s defenses down.

It exploded across the lane, spreading sticky black sludge that clung to Chris and Michael but left the crimson minions untouched.

Tamlin straightened, adjusting his glasses. “Alright, gentlemen,” he called. “Let’s dance.”

Top Lane – Emric and Madi

Emric and Madi got close enough for Emric to focus on one of the Runebreakers. His stomach tightened a little, but he wasn't surprised. In fact, he was almost relieved.

Nia Vale – Crest of Sight. Rank: A

Oh boy, he thought. *Here we go*.

Even through the wards, even from the stands, Emric could *feel* Kael's gaze on them. Watching. Judging.

Beside her, another tag blinked:

Lennox McKinion – Crest of Arcane. Rank: B

Lennox stood higher on a rock, staff glowing faintly. Nia waited below him.

She locked eyes with Emric. Neither moved.

Then Lennox fired a dozen magic missiles. Six aimed for Madi and six for Emric.

They dove apart. The missiles impacting in sequence one after another in a steady line behind them as they ran. They were slow, but Emric could tell they would hurt if they connected.

He rolled, scrambled to his feet, and aimed at Nia. Arcane energy sparked at his fingertips.

But before he could fire, the ground *shook.*

Hard.

The tremor knocked him flat. Madi hit the dirt too. Even Nia stumbled. Lennox looked rattled.

"What was that?"

"Did anyone else feel that?" Tamlin's voice cut in.

"We did in mid," Kennedy said.

Emric's pulse spiked. "Zeb, talk to me. What's going on?"

"I… I don't know," Zeb said, suddenly frantic. "But Beck, Moss, even Principal Grimm, they just stood up. Something is going on."

And then, without warning, the steady *hum* of the arena wards went silent.

Even though it was early morning, the sky went dark.

The shift was instant, like someone had pulled a shroud over the sun. Shadows snapped across the arena, sharp and unnatural, smothering the light.

A thunderous crack followed, splitting the air like the world itself was tearing open.

Above them, every rune across the stadium flickered and died.

The defensive barriers fizzled in jagged sparks and vanished with a hiss. The protective dome that had been there seconds before was simply gone.

The crowd's roar cut off mid-cheer, replaced by confused murmurs that quickly twisted into panic.

In the commentator box, Professor Beck looked around, his usual tired expression wiped clean and replaced with genuine alarm.

Moss sprang to his hooves, eyes darting across the field, scanning for something—anything.

Principal Grimm's gaze narrowed, his jaw tight.

Then came the laugh.

It wasn't sound. Not exactly.

It slithered into their skulls, distorted and wrong, like static caught between radio stations. The pitch wavered—sometimes a growl, sometimes a hiss, sometimes a scream, yet all of it laughing.

All across the stands, people clutched their heads. Some fell to their knees. Others screamed outright.

Then, clear above it all, came the words:

"No more games."

The voice pressed inside their skulls, vibrating against bone. It wasn't coming from the loudspeakers. It was inside them.

Emric spun, eyes wide, searching desperately for the source.

Then the sky ripped open.

A jagged wound of black and pale blue light split the heavens, pulsing with veins of void-fire. Space folded inward like paper crumpling in a fist.

Something fell.

A silhouette plummeted from the wound, trailing fire like a comet.

It hit the arena like a meteor from the heavens.

Stone shattered. Towers disintegrated. Minions, plants, ruins, everything was obliterated in a single shockwave of searing void-flame.

The blast should have killed everyone. It should have wiped the field clean.

But the combatants, the students on both teams, stood untouched in the dust, deliberately spared.

When the smoke finally cleared, the crater glowed in the dead center of the battlefield.

And he stood there.

Tall. Lean. Cloaked in shifting shadows. His hair gleamed like molten silver, spilling to his shoulders. His eyes burned with unnatural pale blue fire. Power radiated from him in crushing waves, the air bending under his presence.

The arena, what was left of it, was silent. No crowd noise. No one moved. No one breathed.

The man raised his head and a slow smile tugged at his mouth.

Then three other figures hit the ground.

Beck. Moss. Grimm.

Three titans of the school stood shoulder to shoulder, mana raging around them.

The intruder tilted his head, amused, as if they were insects trying to hold back a flood.

Then three enormous forms descended from the wound above and slammed down behind him with the weight of mountains.

Void elementals.

Each one towered as tall as the shattered arena walls, their bodies a storm of smoke, claws, and jagged stone. Their eyes glowed with the same pale blue fire as their master's.

The silver-haired man spread his arms like a conductor before an orchestra.

The elementals roared and charged.

With a sound like avalanches breaking loose, the giants thundered forward, claws gouging trenches through the stone. Each step cracked the earth.

Beck flicked his hand and a torrent of lightning tore across the sky. Moss bellowed, horns blazing with nature's fury.

Grimm raised his arm, shadows folding into a blade twice his height.

The arena shook as they clashed.

Shadow, lightning, and wrathfire against the endless hunger of the Void.

The silver-haired man did not move. He stood calm at the center of it all, cloak billowing in the elemental wind, smile tugging faintly at his lips.

Then—without a word—he turned his gaze toward the nearest student.

Kennedy.

His hand rose. Mana coiled.

Beck's eyes widened. He knew what was coming. He raised his hand to counter.

Too late.

The void elemental seized the opening, its massive fist smashing him into the ground.

A spear of searing blue fire shimmered into existence, heat so intense it warped the air around it.

The man let it hover above his palm. Then, with a flick of his wrist, hurled it.

The world slowed.

The spear screamed across the field.

Kennedy froze, paralyzed. Beck was pinned. Emric lunged, but he was too far. Nia gasped.

Kennedy squeezed her eyes shut and braced for the end.

The impact was blinding.

Blue fire erupted, searing the ground. The heat scorched Emric's skin even from across the field.

Kennedy cracked one eye open.

The spear wasn't in her chest. It hovered inches away, stopped.

Pax had thrown himself between her and the spear.

Blue fire punched through stone, through flesh, through soul.

For a single heartbeat, he held.

He looked back at Kennedy, pain twisting his face, and managed a single line:

"Not on my watch."

The silver-haired man clenched his fist.

The spear detonated.

Blue voidfire swallowed Pax whole, tearing stone, flesh, and soul apart.

Kennedy's eyes went wide.

Her scream tore through the arena, raw and broken, as fragments of his stone armor crumbled to dust around her.

Chapter 26

Kennedy's scream still echoed through the arena, ragged and raw, shards of it bouncing off the shattered stone.

She dropped to her knees in the dust where Pax had stood, her fingers scrabbling uselessly through the fragments of his stone armor as if she could piece him back together.

"Pax..." Her voice cracked, high and broken. "You promised..."

The silver-haired man didn't even look at her. His eyes glowed, calm and detached, already shaping another spear.

Kennedy saw it, and something in her snapped.

Her sobbing breath hitched into a furious snarl. She surged to her feet, green light flaring violently around her hands.

"I'm going to rip you limb from limb!" she screamed, shoving her hands forward.

The earth answered. Massive roots erupted from the ground, each one thick as a killer whale, tearing upward in a writhing mass. They raced across the arena and rose like a tidal wave before crashing down toward the silver-haired man.

He tilted his head, mildly curious, then looked away, already bored.

The roots slammed down, the impact shaking the arena to its foundations. Dust boiled into the air. Tears streamed down

Kennedy's face as the roots buried him under tons of crushing wood.

But when the dust settled, he was gone.

Nobody moved. Nobody breathed.

Then he rematerialized. A flicker of shadow, and he was behind her.

The glowing spear stabbed down.

It struck stone instead, sparking violently as Emric barreled through, scooping Kennedy into his arms and carrying her out of the blast. He had never stopped running toward her, not even when Pax's body dissolved.

"KENNEDY!" Madi's voice tore across the field.

Emric landed hard beside her, setting Kennedy down. She clutched at his shirt, sobbing, her eyes hollow as if her soul had been ripped out.

The shockwave rolled across the field, heat clawing at Emric's face as he gritted his teeth against the burn.

Another figure blurred into view. Shaylee, cloak singed, hair wild. She dropped to her knees in front of them, dagger raised and ready.

Madi rounded on Kennedy, fury burning through her grief. "What were you thinking? You want to die too?"

Kennedy just squeezed her eyes tighter shut, another sob breaking loose.

Madi pressed her forehead to hers, voice shaking but steady. "He's gone, Kennedy. He's gone. Don't let him take you too."

Madi held her close, throat tight. Shaylee stayed crouched, blade steady, but even she had gone pale, her mouth pressed in a hard line.

The battlefield roared and burned around them, but in that small circle of broken stone, there was only Kennedy's grief.

The ground shook like an earthquake.

Beck wrenched himself free from the void elemental's crushing grip, arcs of lightning racing down his arms as he forced its fist back with sheer voltage. His jacket hung in tatters, blood streaked his forehead, but his eyes burned sharp and furious.

"Not today!" he roared and drove a stormbolt into the monster's chest. The blast hurled it backward in a spray of rubble, yet it didn't fall. Its torso knit together with smoke and claws, reforming like the wound had been nothing at all.

A second elemental slammed into Moss. The transfiguration professor met it head-on, horns blazing emerald as his hooves carved trenches in the stone. Towering vines erupted from the cracked arena floor, wrapping the beast in choking coils.

"Back to the void with you!" Moss bellowed, each word shaking with fury.

The elemental snarled and tore free, claws shredding the vines like tissue. It lunged, jaws snapping wide enough to swallow him whole. Moss's horns flared brighter, green light erupting into a forest of razor thorns that drove the monster back, but only barely.

The third giant bore down on Grimm.

The principal stood still in its path, his shadow unfurling into a massive blade that towered above him. His eyes glowed like cold iron as the void creature swung.

The clash of claw and shadow sent shockwaves across the arena, each strike loud enough to rattle bones.

Even Grimm, immovable as he seemed, was forced to his knees by the elemental's sheer weight. His blade held, but his jaw tightened, sweat streaking down his temple.

From the stands, terrified screams echoed. Students pressed against the railings. Professors without combat training threw up wards of their own or shielded the youngest, herding them toward the exits, but with the campus wards down, nowhere was safe.

Emric saw it all in flashes as he crouched beside Madi, Shaylee, and Kennedy.

The realization slammed into him.

The professors and the principal weren't winning. They were barely holding the line.

The rest of the faculty had to focus on keeping hundreds of students alive. No reinforcements were coming.

And if even *they* couldn't stop the elementals, what chance did the students have?

The silver-haired man still hadn't moved.

The battle raged around him, but he stood untouched at the center of the battlefield.

His gaze slid past the chaos.

Past the professors.

And settled on Emric.

Emric's stomach clenched. He had known this was coming the moment he pulled Kennedy from the path of the last spear.

Mana coiled around the man's palm again, twisting into another spear, longer and sharper than the first two. Heat bled off it in waves, warping the air like a mirage.

Emric staggered forward, planting himself between his friends and the oncoming strike. His hands flared with arcane light, but compared to the void spear's radiance, it looked pitiful.

Madi braced her staff behind him. Shaylee crouched low, daggers flashing. Kennedy still could not move, tears streaming unchecked down her face.

And Nia, crest blazing, sprinted to her brother's side, eyes blazing with fear and fury.

Even together, they looked so small.

The man smiled faintly and drew his arm back to throw.

Emric's fingers hovered over his belt, ready to smash the trigger on Madi's barrier enchantment. He was not sure it would be enough, but it was the only card left to play.

And then the skyboard above them shattered like glass as a figure dropped from the stands, landing in the dust with a bone-rattling crack.

Kael rose from the crater, cloak shimmering with mana, his eyes burning like his brother's but colder, sharper—carved from iron.

The void spear left the man's hand, screaming toward him.

Kael did not flinch. He raised his arm, conjuring a shield of solid blue mana shaped like a great curved disc, gleaming with raw force.

The spear struck, and Kael deflected it upward with a single brutal motion, knocking it aside like a tennis return. The voidfire shot off its trajectory and streaked skyward, detonating high above the arena in a blossom of pale blue fire. Even at that distance, Emric felt the heat lash across his skin.

"Kael…?" Emric gasped.

His older brother didn't even look at him.

Kael stepped between Emric and the silver-haired man, stance unshakable. His voice rang out, flat and absolute.

"You don't touch him."

The silver-haired man tilted his head, and for the first time, his smile widened.

"Hey, Frosted Flake, did you wander in from your shift at Hot Topic?"

"Ah," he said softly, "the knight in shining armor appears."

With another flick of his fingers, a new spear shimmered into being.

Nia raised her fingers. Her crest blazed, threads of light weaving across her fingers like constellations. She whispered, and the air itself bent.

The man hurled his spear. It shrieked forward and curved.

To his own eyes, the void spear twisted in mid-flight like a boomerang and slammed back into his chest. The blast staggered him a full step, cloak tearing, voidfire spraying the air.

But no one else saw the spear. To the crowd, to the professors, even to Emric and Kael, it looked like the silver-haired man suddenly recoiled from an invisible strike, as though some unseen hand had forced him back.

He looked down at his ribs, breath ragged, smile faltering. His gaze snapped to Nia, realization dawning.

"Clever trick, young one," he murmured, his voice calm but edged with heat. He had seen through it, but not before it rattled him.

Emric didn't wait. He thrust both hands forward, arcane power spiraling into a violet blast that cracked against the man's guard.

Blood sprayed, and the man's eyes went wide. His lips moved, voice low and almost disbelieving.

"He said I couldn't get hurt."

His eyes darkened, furious now, the faintest tremor in his tone.

"He lied to me."

Kael surged immediately after, mana flaring in his grip. A giant warhammer of pure light crystallized in his hands, heavy and radiant. He swung it down with crushing force.

For the first time since their mother's death, all three Vale siblings stood together. Three different crests, three different strengths, all converging on one enemy.

And for the first time – together they struck.

Kael's warhammer crashed down, the arena floor buckling under the impact. Emric's arcane blast still burned at the man's ribs. Nia's spell-thread shimmered through the air like starlight, weaving confusion into his senses.

For a moment, it looked like it was working.

The man staggered, cloak torn by the arcane blast, voidfire spraying in jagged arcs. His smile was gone now, his breath uneven.

Emric's mind raced. He had drawn blood, and if he could bleed, he could be beaten.

But the moment was fragile. Already the man's stance shifted, his eyes sharpening.

Around them, the professors were still locked in their own battles. Beck writhed under a colossal fist, lightning sparking desperately across his arms. Moss was buried under torn vines, horns blazing green as he tried to keep the beast back. Grimm's blade rang against claws the size of carriages, each strike shaking the arena.

The faculty were overwhelmed. This left the siblings alone.

The intruder straightened. Shadows coiled around his body, knitting into place. His eyes burned hotter, fixed on Emric.

"You," the man said softly, almost curious. "You hurt me."

Blood still clung to his ribs where Emric's Arcane Blast had scored a clean strike.

Void mana coiled around his hands, brighter than before.

Arcane Bulwark.

The whisper rushed through Emric's head. He didn't hesitate. He slammed his hand down on his buckler, and Madi's enchantment flared around him in a dome of violet light.

For a heartbeat, hope surged. The barrier hummed strong and solid.

Then the void lightning struck.

It pierced the Bulwark like a hot knife through butter.

The blast tore through Emric's chest. For an instant, his whole body glowed from within, brighter than the sun, then the light collapsed inward, swallowing him whole.

Chapter 27

Kael had seen his brother take hits before, mostly from him. Crushing blows, explosions, sparring mishaps, he had watched Emric stumble, bleed, and get back up every time.

But never like this.

The void lightning tore through Emric's enchanted shield and into his chest, and for one impossible instant, Kael swore the world itself stopped. His little brother glowed from within the barrier, brighter than the sun, then folded inward as if the light had been swallowed whole.

And then he fell.

"Emric!" Kael's voice ripped out of him, raw and ragged. He lunged forward, boots skidding on shattered stone, too far away to catch him before his body collapsed in a lifeless heap.

Nia screamed. So did Madi. Shaylee's daggers slipped from her grasp. Tamlin stood frozen, pale and speechless.

Kael's chest hollowed in a way he had never felt before. He had sworn by his life that nothing would touch his siblings while he was there. That was his role. His burden. His promise.

And now Emric lay still on the battlefield, smoke curling from his chest where the blast had torn through.

The silver-haired man didn't even pause. He turned lazily, voidfire curling in his palm as if he had merely swatted an insect out of his way.

This wasn't real. This couldn't be happening. First Mom. Now Emric. His family was breaking piece by piece, and he was powerless to stop it.

Pax's name caught in his throat. The man had already killed Emric's teammate, Pax, who had stood in front of Kennedy when no one else could. And now he had taken Emric too.

Kael's vision blurred red.

He roared, his warhammer blazing in his grip, and hurled himself at the man. The impact rattled the arena like thunder, each swing fueled not by discipline but by rage. His mana shield flared as claws of voidfire lashed toward him. He didn't care. He couldn't allow this monster to continue. He had to protect the only family he had left.

But even rage couldn't hide the truth. Kael was being pushed back. Step by step, the man's voidfire cut deeper, forcing him onto his heels.

Somewhere behind him, he heard Nia trying desperately to anchor her divination threads into his strikes, weaving omens and foresight, but her focus cracked again and again. Madi slammed barriers into place, her staff sparking with energy. Shaylee, face streaked with tears, darted like a shadow for the man's back, only to be blown away by a careless flick of void energy.

They were holding on, barely. Their spells flew, their blades flashed, but their rhythm was broken. How could they focus when Emric's body still smoked on the stone between them?

Kael swatted away another spear. His shield shattered. His arms trembled with the force, teeth gritted as he forced himself upright.

And then, through the chaos, another sound cut through.

A voice.

Darian's voice.

Kael's head snapped sideways. For a heartbeat, he thought he was imagining it. His father, the man who hadn't moved or lifted a hand this whole time, was suddenly there beside Nia, kneeling over Emric's body.

Mana poured from him in waves. Not a stream but a flood. A torrent. Radiant and overwhelming, like a dam finally giving way after years of pressure.

The ground itself glowed with it.

Kael's chest clenched. He didn't dare believe it. Not yet. But—

"Dad…?" he whispered, even as the silver-haired man conjured another spear, his burning eyes fixed on Kael, a sinister smile curving his lips.

Darian's hands hovered above Emric's chest, fingers spread wide. The torrent of mana spilling from him was nothing Kael had ever felt before, dense and searing, almost alive.

It wasn't just light. It was weight. The air bent under it, pressing against skin and stone alike.

Kael's lungs seized as he felt the ripple across the battlefield. And it wasn't just him.

Madi gasped as her staff flared brighter, the runes along its shaft blazing with new force. Kennedy's head lifted from where she had been sobbing, drawn toward the glow. Shaylee's daggers, dim a moment ago, gleamed sharp with renewed enchantment. Even Nia's foresight threads straightened, no longer flickering but weaving smooth and steady, like static clearing to a perfect signal.

The professors felt it too.

Beck's lightning roared louder as he forced himself upright, hair standing wild from the surge. Moss's eyes and horns burned like emerald fire, his roots surging thicker and faster as they bound the elemental again. Grimm's shadow-blade stretched taller and sharper, shrieking as it clashed against claws like steel torn from the earth.

It was all residual, all bleed-off.

Darian wasn't even trying to strengthen them. Every drop of mana he poured into Emric overflowed, spilling across the arena like a rising tide.

And even that overflow was enough to steady them. Enough to remind them they weren't beaten yet.

Kael dragged in a ragged breath. His shield immediately reformed and knocked the incoming spear right back at the man.

The man dodged out of the way, barely making it, and half of his hair was burnt away from his own redirected attack.

Kael set his jaw, heat roaring back through his chest. "Alright ya Frosted Flake. Here comes round two."

He charged.

Madi's barriers slammed into place beside him, stronger and sharper than before. Shaylee darted through his shadow, her daggers sparking like stars. Nia's voice rang clear, her foresight laying constellations of light across the ground. And Kennedy, hands still trembling and eyes hollow, lifted them anyway, forcing healing light through her grief, pouring her strength into Darian's desperate work.

The professors rallied. Beck's storm split the sky. Moss's roots choked the elemental in a net of thorns. Grimm's shadow-blade howled as it cleaved into void flesh again and again.

For the first time since Pax's fall, since Emric's collapse, the battlefield pushed back.

And through it all, Darian did not move. Bent over Emric's body, jaw clenched, sweat streaking his temples. His hands never wavered. His torrent never slowed.

Every ounce of his power was fixed on one thing.

Bringing his son back.

Chapter 28

Silence.

Emric's eyes snapped open. His breath caught.

The arena was gone.

He stood in a wide-open field, grass brushing his legs in waves of green and gold. Wildflowers dotted the hillsides, bending gently in the breeze. The sky above was endless blue, so clear it hurt to look at. Birds wheeled overhead, their songs carrying sweet and calm on the air.

It was beautiful. Too beautiful.

His heart hammered. This wasn't right. He'd been in the arena. His chest still remembered the pain—the blast ripping through him, Madi's Bulwark shattering like glass.

His hands flew to his ribs. Whole. No wound. No blood.

Confusion tangled in his throat. He turned in a circle, searching for something—anything familiar. A landmark. A tower. A sound of battle. But there was nothing.

And then he saw her.

A figure in the distance, walking slowly toward him. Sunlight haloed her, golden on her hair.

Emric froze. His breath came sharp and shallow.

"No..." His voice cracked. "This isn't possible."

But she kept walking, her steps steady and graceful.

Closer now. Close enough that he could see her face.

His mother.

The word wasn't enough. It didn't even begin to hold what hit him.

"Mom..." The sound tore out of him like a sob.

His legs moved before he realized it, pounding across the grass. His vision blurred, hot tears streaming down his face. For one raw, unguarded instant, he wasn't a crest-bearer, wasn't a fighter in a tournament.

He was a child again.

He threw his arms around her, burying his face into her shoulder.

Her arms wrapped him up—warm, steady, real. She smelled like their old home in New York, something he hadn't realized he'd missed so much.

The dam inside him broke. He sobbed into her, clutching her like he could keep her from slipping away this time.

"I'm so sorry, Mom," he choked, words tangled and desperate. "I didn't mean to get you killed—I'm so sorry."

Her hands cupped the back of his head, pulling him tighter against her shoulder.

“Oh, Emric…” Her voice was soft, steady, the kind that had soothed scraped knees and nightmares. “No. No, sweetheart. You didn’t get me killed.”

She leaned back just enough to meet his eyes, her thumbs brushing away his tears even as more spilled. Her gaze was warm and unshakable, her smile tinged with sadness but fierce with love.

“That was never on you. Not then. Not ever.”

She brushed her thumb across his cheek, her smile soft but unshakable. “Even if I could turn back time, Emric… some things are out of our hands.”

The words hit him harder than the blast had. His throat closed, a fresh sob tearing out of him as he clung tighter.

He cried until his throat ached, until his chest felt raw, until the sobs finally thinned into jagged breaths. For long minutes, she just held him, stroking his hair like she had when he was small—steady and patient.

At last, he managed to speak, his voice hoarse and trembling.

“Am I… dead?” He pulled back enough to search her face, panic and hope warring in his eyes. “If you’re here, and I’m here—then that’s it, right? I died.”

She shook her head gently, brushing his cheek with her hand.

“Not yet. Not fully. That could still change.” Her eyes softened, but there was weight behind them. “The blast should have killed you, Emric. But thanks to your friend

Madi's enchantment—the Arcane Bulwark—it absorbed just enough to keep it from being final. You're in the in-between now. Balance could tip either way. But if I know your father, he'll be fixing that shortly."

His breath caught. His mind scrambled to keep up.

"How… how do you know about Madi?" he asked, voice cracking.

Her smile was faint, wistful. "Because I've been with you the whole time."

Emric blinked. His stomach dropped.

She tilted her head, golden hair catching the light. "I'm glad I told you to use your Arcane Bulwark when I did."

The realization hit like lightning. His pulse roared in his ears.

"The Whisper…" he whispered.

Her eyes shone, proud and sad all at once. "Yes. That was me."

Emric blinked at her, still trying to make sense of any of it. His voice shook. "I don't… I don't get it. If you're dead, and I'm not… how can this be real? How am I here with you?"

Her smile deepened, sad but certain. "Oh, it's real all right. You can thank your ancestors for that."

"Ancestors?"

She nodded, releasing him gently so she could gesture to the vast sky and the endless rolling fields around them. "The Legacy spell. It's a covenant—one passed down through our bloodline for generations. A protection, a whisper, a guiding voice when the bearer is ready."

Emric swallowed. "Did Dad know?"

Her expression shifted, heavy with regret. "No. I always meant to tell him… I just never knew how. And then, time ran out."

Emric's throat tightened. "Then why me? Shouldn't you have given it to Kael? He was older… stronger… more ready than I'll ever be."

Her face softened, guilt and something else flickering in her eyes. "The truth is… I hadn't decided yet. None of you were ready. Not Kael. Not you. Not Nia."

She hesitated, voice softening. "But I'll admit—I was leaning toward you. I saw something in you."

Emric blinked. His chest tightened. "A spark?"

Her lips curved, faint but real. "Yeah. I even told Darian that once, late one night."

Emric's heart jolted. "He told me… and then Kael mentioned something."

She laughed quietly, a sound like sunlight cutting through the weight between them. "I always wondered if my intuition was right—that Kael had been eavesdropping on that conversation."

Her smile faded as her hand brushed his cheek again, trembling now. "But that night—when it all happened—even though it wasn't your fault, I had to make a choice. And I only had one option. You. So I gave it to you before I died."

Her hand lingered on him, warm and steady. "It wasn't fair. You've been carrying this without knowing it. And I am so sorry for that. But…" She drew a deep breath, eyes shimmering. "I'm grateful you were there that night. Either way, I wasn't getting out alive. But because you were there, the power continued. Without you, it would've died with me."

The words hit Emric like a weight dropped straight onto his chest.

He staggered back a half-step, his breath shuddering. His whole life, he'd carried that night like a scar carved into his soul. The guilt, the shame, the helplessness—he'd replayed it a thousand times, always ending with the same truth: *he hadn't been enough to* save her.

But now—now she was telling him that wasn't the truth at all.

Tears blurred his vision, spilling hot down his face. His knees buckled, sinking into the wildflowers, his hands digging into the earth. The sob broke free before he could stop it, raw and shaking.

“All this time…” His voice cracked. “I thought I failed you. I thought if I’d been faster, stronger—if I’d just done something— I just froze.”

She knelt in front of him, her hand cupping his face, firm enough to steady him.

“You didn’t fail me, Emric,” she whispered. “You saved something greater than me. You carried forward what I couldn’t. My death wasn’t your fault. But the Legacy still lives because of you.”

Emric squeezed his eyes shut, clinging to her words like a lifeline. His chest ached—but the ache wasn’t guilt anymore. It was release.

Her thumb brushed the tear streak from his cheek, her voice soft but steady.

“Listen to me, Emric—we don’t have long. I can feel your father casting his regeneration spells, so you should be back soon. But I need you to hear this.”

Her eyes shone brighter now, as though the sunlight itself poured through them. “The Legacy isn’t just a whisper. It’s a covenant—an inheritance of every bearer before you. Each of us, across generations, tied to different crests. Chain. Wards. Veil. Mind. Essence. Bloom. My gift was the Elements. And now…”

“Yours is Arcane. Which means you carry them all—the ones I named, and others still to come. They live in you now. Every spell. Every gift. Every burden. Not perfectly. Not without practice. But they are there. And you must train, discipline yourself—or the power will break you before it makes you."

"And now that you know… your Arcane will awaken in ways it never could before. Stronger. Wilder. More dangerous. But don't rely on it alone. The Legacy offers more than raw strength. Arcane is the key that binds them. Master it—and the others will follow."

Emric's throat went dry. "But… if that's true—why me? Why now?"

Her smile trembled, proud and guilty all at once. "Because I didn't have a choice. You were all too young. But that night, I knew I wouldn't survive. If I let the Legacy die with me, our family's line of power would end forever. You were there, Emric. So I gave it to you. Too early. Before I was ready. Before you were ready."

Emric's voice wavered. "I don't understand… if this Legacy is supposed to protect us, why didn't it protect you?"

Her face softened, sorrow threading through her smile. She brushed her thumb against his cheek, shaking her head.

"Remember this, Emric. The Legacy protects what we are. But it doesn't stop death. It was never meant to."

Her expression darkened, urgency sparking in her eyes. "There is a man who hunts our family for this power—he's been searching for the Legacy for longer than any normal person should be allowed to live. Always chasing. Always killing. He is getting closer, Emric."

He felt his stomach drop. "The man in the arena."

Her expression hardened. She shook her head. "Not him. I don't know who he is. But the one who hunts you is getting close. And if he finds you, if he rips the Legacy from you, it won't just kill you—he will destroy everyone you love. Everyone."

The wind around them grew louder. Her form shimmered faintly, like she was becoming light itself.

She clutched his face one last time, her eyes fierce even through the sorrow. "So, you must live. Train. Endure. And trust Kael. Trust Nia. Trust your friends. The Legacy isn't meant to be carried alone. I learned that the hard way."

Her lips brushed his forehead. "I love you, Emric. Always. No matter what comes."

The field shattered. His mother's warmth slipped away—

And Emric gasped back to life, choking on ash and fire.

Chapter 29

Ash scorched his lungs. Light seared behind his eyelids.

Emric gasped, his body arching off the stone like he'd been hit with defibrillator paddles made of molten lightning. He coughed hard—his chest spasming as the first breath tore through him like broken glass. The world snapped into focus, chaos screaming around him.

Screaming. Roaring. Stone cracking under colossal weight. Spells detonating. Magic ripping through the air.

Heat lashed his skin in waves.

He blinked, eyes adjusting to a battlefield that looked nothing like the arena he remembered. Most of the platforms were gone—collapsed or obliterated. Shattered towers bled mana like rivers. One of the void elementals tore through the stands like a wrecking ball.

Before he could get lost in the chaos, someone gripped his shoulder. Warm. Real.

Emric turned.

His father was kneeling beside him, one hand still gripping his shoulder, the other hovering over his chest, light flickering faintly between his fingers. He looked like he'd just crawled out of a bomb crater—cloak burned, eyes wild, breathing ragged.

“Dad...” Emric croaked.

Then Darian pulled him into the tightest hug he’d ever given. His voice cracked against Emric’s ear.

“I’m so sorry, Emric.”

And just like that—Emric knew.

That hadn’t been a dream. His mom had been right.

His father had come for him.

The warmth in his chest wasn’t just healing. It was recognition. Of power. Of legacy. Of love.

Still dazed, Emric let out a shaky breath and rasped, “Hey, Dad.”

Darian pulled back, eyes scanning him like he wasn’t sure whether to laugh or cry. His voice came low and hoarse:

“Hey, Son.”

“I need to tell you something—”

Darian cut him off, voice calm but clipped:

“Save it for later, Emric. We’re kind of busy right now.”

Emric blinked and looked around.

Kael was still fighting the silver-haired man. The battle was still raging.

He’d been so deep in his own head, he’d forgotten the world was ending.

CRASH

One of the void elementals hurled Moss through a support tower fifty yards away.

Darian stood and offered a hand. Emric took it and pulled himself to his feet, face turned toward the chaos.

His legs felt like soggy noodles. His chest still burned. But beneath it all, he could feel it—the **Arcane**, humming inside him.

Hotter. Brighter. Stronger than it had ever been.

He looked past the smoke and rubble.

Kael's warhammer swung in wide arcs.

Nia's foresight threads shimmered with perfect clarity.

Madi and Shaylee flanked them, blades and spells blazing.

Kennedy stood behind them, hands glowing emerald, grief burning in her eyes.

His friends. His family.

Still fighting.

Emric drew a breath, turned to Darian, and smiled faintly.

"Don't worry, Dad," he said, teeth gritted, eyes hard.

"I've got this."

Then he ran.

Kael's warhammer slammed into the earth, throwing up shards of broken stone as the man danced back a step—his mouth curved in a smile like he was simply playing with them.

The rhythm of the fight was turning brutal. Kael was alone up front. Nia was repositioning.

The villain readied another spear—aimed directly at Nia.

Then—

CRACK

A blast of blue-violet Arcane energy slammed into the man from the side, detonating in a ripple of warped light. The blast didn't just impact him—it sent him rocketing backward, feet skidding on the ground, but still upright.

Everyone turned.

Emric was running full speed into the fight.

His hands flared, and the moment his feet hit the stone, another burst of Arcane power surged from his palm. This one missing the target, it looked like Emric was stumbling off balance like he wasn't prepared for the pushback of his own spell.

Madi covered her mouth in disbelief. Shaylee gasped. Kennedy's eyes flickered with hope when she saw him. Nia jumped up and down, excited. The student who moments ago had been dead on the ground was now alive, but was running back into the fight that had killed him.

Emric slid to a stop near his older brother.

"What took you so long?" Kael said sarcastically.

"Oh, you know… just catching up with mom," Emric replied casually.

Nia and Kael looked at him like he was going crazy.

"I'll tell you later," he said with a grin.

The man staggered to a halt, staring at Emric like he was seeing a ghost. His side was bloody where Emric's latest Arcane Blast had struck.

His voice low and tense: "Is this a joke?"

Emric lowered his stance, mana arcing between his fingers. "Did you miss me?"

"Are you making fun of me?"

He didn't wait for an answer, readying another spear.

Emric braced himself, preparing for the more powerful pushback, and launched an Arcane Missile straight at the man's hand. The blast tore through his wrist—his hand vanished in a red vapor, blood erupting like a geyser.

Emric's eyes went wide. He hadn't meant to do that.

Mom wasn't kidding.

The man screamed and cast a spell, stopping the blood flow, fury etched into his face.

He staggered back, eyes wild, one hand now sealed in black crystal where his wrist had been. A low, guttural, inhuman snarl twisted from his throat.

Then he raised his one remaining hand.

A ping of void mana spread throughout the arena. Far across the field, the elementals froze. Grimm's blade struck empty air as his opponent turned mid-strike. Moss, covered in vines and blood, lurched backward as the one grappling him suddenly withdrew. Beck flared with lightning—only to watch his enemy step away as if none of them mattered.

Three towering shadows turned.

And in unison, the three behemoths let out a roar and charged.

Stone cracked under every step. Claws raked the earth. One let out a screech that Emric could feel in his bones.

"Oh boy," Kael's eyes widened.

Before anyone could move—

Something small arced high above the battlefield.

A glint of glass, barely visible against the void-covered sky. It spun as it flew—a perfect, calculated throw—and reached the apex directly above the three charging elementals.

For a second, no one noticed. The monsters didn't even look up.

Then—

BOOM

A blinding explosion of light detonated midair.

It wasn't fire. It wasn't lightning. It was pure white brilliance, like someone had cracked the sun like an egg and dropped it straight onto the field.

The elementals screeched and skidded to a halt, claws slamming into stone as the light overloaded their senses. Shadows thrashed wildly around them. Even the silver-haired man shielded his eyes, staggering back a step.

When the glow faded—

Tamlin was standing at the front of the student line.

Grinning.

Shaylee stepped up beside him, her twin daggers gleaming like stars.

Madi followed, staff already humming.

Kennedy stood tall, healing light flaring at her palms, eyes locked on the nearest elemental.

"Sorry I took so long," Tamlin said. "I was stuck under half a tower. Yelled for help—but y'know, *apocalypse noise.*"

"But you're here now," Emric finished for him.

"Did you like that?" Tamlin said. "My own blend of flash rune. I think I'll call it *Suns Out, Claws Out.*"

Kael didn't even flinch. "You're an idiot."

The ground started to shake; the elementals were back to their senses and charging.

One crashed between Emric and the others, swinging a jagged arm like a wrecking ball. The blast of impact sent Emric stumbling left, forced to roll under a second swipe that shattered a platform behind him.

A second elemental cut off Kael and Nia, slamming its fists down like meteors. The siblings barely dodged, Kael grabbing Nia's arm and pulling her behind him as rubble exploded around them.

The third screeched and barreled straight toward Tamlin's group.

The battlefield shattered into chaos again.

Across the field, the professors struggled to sit up.

Beck's arms sparked weakly as he tried to raise his hands, refusing to let his students fight alone. His chest convulsed, blood flecking his lips, and he slumped back against the wall with a groan.

Grimm's massive shadowblade flickered in and out of existence, his grip faltering, knees shaking like the ground beneath him.

Moss slumped against a shattered column, vines crawling sluggishly over his body in a desperate attempt to stitch his wounds closed. The effort left him trembling, sweat running in rivulets down his brow.

They weren't unconscious—yet.

Every drop of mana, every ounce of strength, had gone into holding the line.

Darian ran to them, nearly tripping on broken stone. His cloak whipped behind him as he dropped to a knee beside Moss, already casting.

"Still alive?" he asked breathlessly.

Grimm gave a weak grunt. "Barely."

Darian didn't waste words. He raised his hands. Mana pulsed from his palms—not the torrent he'd poured into Emric, but steady, controlled, relentless.

Moss's vines retreated back into the earth as the wounds sealed. Grimm's blade steadied, solid once more. Beck straightened, wiping blood from his mouth, sparks around his hands flaring brighter.

None of them were at full strength. Not even close. But they could stand again.

And for now, that was enough.

The battlefield was fire and shadow.

The elemental thundered down on Tamlin's group, claws raking trenches through the stone.

Madi's barrier cracked, spiderwebs of light spreading across its surface. Shaylee darted low, her daggers slashing at tendons that reformed instantly. Kennedy poured healing magic into them, her face pale and wet with sweat.

Tamlin hurled another vial, the glass shattering into flame against the void. It staggered, hissed, then came on harder.

"We are not—" Tamlin gasped, rolling as its fist smashed where he'd stood a second earlier, "—losing to this thing!"

"Then we need to think of something," Shaylee shot back, "because if this keeps up, we are not going to win."

Across the field, Kael and Nia stood shoulder-to-shoulder.

Nia's foresight threads burned bright, weaving paths of possible futures in quicksilver arcs around them.

"Right side!" she shouted.

Kael swung his hammer into the elemental's claw, the impact cracking like thunder. The blow hurled it back a step, but he dug in, bracing his shield as the beast pressed harder.

They were holding. Barely. Neither side could gain the edge.

Nia's eyes glowed with strain. "I don't know how much longer I can keep this up!"

"Then we need to finish this now," Kael growled, jaw tight as he shoved back with all his strength.

Emric faced his alone.

The elemental lunged, claws like blades, screaming through the air.

And somehow… he was already moving.

He didn't see the strike coming so much as he felt it—a pull in his gut, a pulse in his blood. His body moved before his mind caught up, twisting aside as the claw ripped through empty space.

Another blow came down, and again, his body reacted first. His hands lifted, mana already flaring before the attack even fell. He dove through the gap, rolled, and fired an Arcane Blast into the elemental's exposed side.

The blast seared a crater of violet across its ribs. The monster staggered.

And then he understood.

It wasn't him. Not exactly.

It was her.

His mother's Crest—the Elements—alive in his blood through the Legacy. He could feel the elemental the way she would have. Its weight. Its momentum. Its intent.

Every strike carried a rhythm, and that rhythm thrummed inside his bones like a second heartbeat.

The elemental roared, lashing again.

He didn't retreat; he stepped in, closer, inside the arc of the claws slashing down.

He slipped sideways, the blow missing by inches, and thrust his arms outward with incredible velocity.

Arcane Explosion.

The blast tore the void creature into ribbons. His most powerful Arcane attack at point-blank range was too much for even the elemental to withstand. It dissolved into smoke and shreds of shadow, its roar breaking apart into a dying hiss.

The remaining two elementals turned at the sound of their comrade's death.

Their hollow eyes locked on Emric. Their roars split the air in unison, the ground trembling as both titans abandoned their opponents and charged straight for him.

"Emric!" Shaylee screamed.

Kael's hammer crushed the ground in front of him, but the elemental moved past him, fixated on Emric. It didn't even glance at Kael.

Thinking quickly, Tamlin grabbed another vial. Shaylee and Madi sprinted toward Emric's flank. Kennedy's hands blazed green as she forced more mana into the team, her face tight with strain.

The elementals converged.

Claws the size of boulders slashed down—

—but Emric was already moving.

He slipped through the gap as though it were a rehearsed dance. Each strike missed by millimeters, ripping stone apart but never touching him. His movements weren't desperate; they were instinctive, precise, almost calm.

The others didn't waste the opening.

"Come on!" Kael roared.

His warhammer blazed as he drove it into one elemental's knee, shattering the joint in a blast of force. Nia's foresight threads coiled around the second, guiding Shaylee's daggers into its exposed tendons, every strike perfectly timed.

Madi slammed her staff into the earth—a wall of violet force erupted, pinning one monster against the wreckage of a fallen tower. Kennedy flared with light, pouring strength into Kael as he struggled against the elemental's raw power, pushing him past his natural breaking point.

Emric didn't even blink at the chaos. He simply would not allow the elementals to touch him, drawing their full attention with every untouchable movement.

Tamlin leapt onto the back of one of the elementals and smashed his vial against the base of its skull. He jumped off just as a bright white liquid oozed over its head like holy acid, burning against the void.

"Keep going, kids," Darian said softly from a distance.

The students became a storm. Every blow landed harder than the last, every spell tearing deeper. The elementals clawed for Emric again, but he was untouchable, a blur weaving through their strikes.

The one Tamlin had splashed collapsed under the combined assault, its body ripping apart in vapors of smoke. The other staggered back, riddled with concussive hammer blows and flashing dagger strikes, until Kael's final swing smashed through its skull in a thunderous crack.

Silence.

The last void elemental crumbled, dissolving into ribbons of smoke carried away by the wind.

Kael straightened, chest heaving, warhammer dragging at his side. He wiped a streak of blood from his mouth and looked back at the others.

"Alright," he panted, forcing a grin. "Now for the big boss man."

They turned.

The silver-haired man was gone.

The battlefield where he had stood was empty—only cracked stone and drifting ash. No trail. No sound.

Nia's eyes widened. "He... he was here the whole time. How did he—"

"He slipped away," Kael said grimly, the grin gone. "Used his pets to cover his retreat."

Emric's pulse still raced from the fight, his body humming with inherited power, but his stomach sank as he realized the truth.

They hadn't won. Not really.

The monster who did this, who killed Pax—

—was still out there.

Kennedy dropped to her knees, hands shaking as she gathered shards of stone armor scattered across the ground—the last pieces of him. She pressed one jagged piece to her chest, as if sheer force of will could anchor him back to her.

Her lips trembled. "You promised..." she whispered.

Madi went over and simply held Kennedy while she sobbed.

Emric clenched his fists until his nails bit into his palms.

They had survived the fight.

But they had not won.

Chapter 30

Two weeks later

The Academy grounds still smelled of smoke. Even after endless cleansing spells, ash clung to the stone, lodged in every crack, soaked into every surface. Where the arena had once stood proud, there was now only a crater—jagged stone and broken wards stitched over by scaffolds and glowing rune-lattices.

The Pillar of Preservation had arrived within minutes of the battle's end, stabilizing the wounded with spells older than the Academy itself. The Pillar of Authority was there as well, locking down the school, sealing the skies above with new barriers, their presence heavy and unyielding.

Dozens of students had been hospitalized. When the wards collapsed, panic and rubble had torn through the stands, crushing or scattering anyone caught too close.

Zeb had been one of them.

He hadn't been on the battlefield—Professor Jenkins had tried to usher him out when the wards broke. But a falling beam of enchanted stone had pinned him before he could escape. He'd lain there unconscious through the entire battle, barely clinging to life until a preservation mage found him.

He survived. But only just.

Classes had been suspended. The tournament was canceled. For two weeks, the Academy was closed to allow recovery—both physical and emotional—for those involved. The Pillar of Enlightenment offered free grief counseling to anyone affected by the event.

The Academy would recover. But its innocence was gone.

And today, so were the students.

Today wasn't about repairs. Or lessons.

Today was about Pax.

The funeral was held on the Academy's western lawn, where the mountains framed the horizon, and the wind carried the sound of bells down from the spires.

Rows of white chairs had been set up on the grass, but most people stood: students in uniform, faculty in solemn robes.

At the front, a blackstone plinth bore Pax's crest, engraved and still glowing faintly. A wreath of wildflowers had been laid around it—Kennedy's doing. She had gathered them herself, refusing to let anyone else.

The air was quiet, save for murmurs of grief and the rustle of robes in the breeze.

Principal Grimm spoke first, his voice as steady as always, though it carried a weight Emric had never heard before.

"Pax Carroway gave his life not in duty, nor in obligation, but in choice. He chose to stand between a friend and death itself. There is no higher courage. There is no greater legacy."

He cleared his throat, tears in his eyes as he spoke. "We will heal. We will rebuild. But we will never forget the boy who stood when no one else could. Pax will remain with us—in our memory, and in the strength we find from his example. Let no one here doubt: he mattered. His choice mattered. And as long as we speak his name, he is not gone."

His words hung in the air as the silence continued.

Then one by one, they came forward.

Kennedy pressed the rose against the plinth, then broke. Madi moved instantly, wrapping her arms around her as Kennedy sobbed into her shoulder.

Everyone who knew and loved Pax paid their respects.

Emric stood next to Kael and Nia, his arms silently crossed as she held onto Emric's arm.

The bells tolled—low, heavy, final.

The service ended in silence. No applause. No grand declarations. Just the wind moving through the grass and the sound of Kennedy's quiet sobs as her friends stood around her, refusing to let her stand alone.

Epilogue

Far from the academy, the night was silent.

A ruined chapel stood on the cliffs, its roof collapsed, its walls blackened by fire. Inside, shadows curled like smoke around a figure slumped against the altar.

The silver-haired man.

His cloak hung in tatters, one sleeve torn away, his right wrist sealed in black crystal where his hand had once been. Blood streaked down his jaw, but his pale eyes still burned—not with defeat but with a simmering rage.

He stared at the empty air for a long moment, breathing ragged. Then he laughed. Low. Bitter.

"They hurt me," he whispered. His voice cracked between disbelief and fury. "You lied to me, Master."

He pressed his left hand against his ribs, where Emric's Arcane Blast had torn through him. Even now, the wound smoldered, refusing to close.

The chapel's shadows deepened, pooling unnaturally at his feet. From that blackness, a whisper rose—not his own. Cold. Ancient. Patient.

"You faced the boy. You saw it, didn't you? The Legacy lives within him."

The man's jaw tightened. His silver hair fell loose across his face.

"Yes," he growled. "But he is clumsy. Weak. Not ready." His voice dipped, guttural. "Next time, it will be yours."

The voice in the dark spoke again, slow and hollow.

"Do not be so certain. You lost today, and I have waited longer than you can imagine. That spell is mine, and soon... I will take my sister's gift back to where it rightfully belongs."

The shadows thinned, leaving only silence and the man's ragged breathing.

He tilted his head back against the altar, pale eyes burning against the ceiling's void.

"Enjoy your victory, boy," he murmured. His mouth twisted into a faint, feral smile.

"We're coming for you."

www.ingramcontent.com/pod-product-compliance
Lightning Source LLC
Chambersburg PA
CBHW070638310726
48982CB00001B/318

* 9 7 9 8 9 0 2 5 4 9 9 4 9 *